"What objections can you possibly have to this marriage?"

"What objections?" A chill ran over her like an icy finger down her spine, straight into her soul, chilling her right through. She *knew* that voice. Oh, how she knew that voice. It was the voice that had haunted her dreams, when she'd woken up in tangled sheets, gasping with a potent mix of desire, hope and fear. A roughened thrum, shot through with a velvety softness, a hint of laughter lurking somewhere deep within the assured rumble, it was a voice that conjured so many memories, and too many regrets. A voice that had made her smile, even when she hadn't wanted it to. *Hold on to your senses, Emma. Head over heels is definitely not for you.* It was a voice she'd never, ever expected to hear again, because its owner was dead.

"My objection," the owner of that silky, powerful voice continued, coming to the front of the church, a shaft of sunlight from the stained glass above gilding his dark hair in gold, barely leashed fury emanating from every powerful line of his taut body, "is that the bride is already married. To me."

After spending three years as a die-hard New Yorker, **Kate Hewitt** now lives in a small village in the English Lake District with her husband, their five children and a golden retriever. In addition to writing intensely emotional stories, she loves reading, baking and playing chess with her son— she has yet to win against him, but she continues to try. Learn more about Kate at kate-hewitt.com.

Books by Kate Hewitt

Harlequin Presents

Claiming My Bride of Convenience
Vows to Save His Crown
Pride & the Italian's Proposal

Passionately Ever After...

A Scandal Made at Midnight

One Night with Consequences

Princess's Nine-Month Secret
Greek's Baby of Redemption

Secret Heirs of Billionaires

The Secret Kept from the Italian
The Italian's Unexpected Baby

Visit the Author Profile page
at Harlequin.com for more titles.

Kate Hewitt

———

BACK TO CLAIM HIS ITALIAN HEIR

HARLEQUIN
PRESENTS

Recycling programs for this product may not exist in your area.

ISBN-13: 978-1-335-73943-8

Back to Claim His Italian Heir

Copyright © 2023 by Kate Hewitt

For questions and comments about the quality of this book, please contact us at CustomerService@Harlequin.com.

Harlequin Enterprises ULC
22 Adelaide St. West, 41st Floor
Toronto, Ontario M5H 4E3, Canada
www.Harlequin.com

Printed in U.S.A.

BACK TO CLAIM HIS
ITALIAN HEIR

For Jenna, who has been with me all the way!
Love, K.

CHAPTER ONE

'I DO.'

The words ringing out through the church were not the ones Emma Dunnett expected. They weren't the ones *anyone* expected, because this was the part of the wedding ceremony where everybody was meant to stay deliberately, determinedly silent, without so much as a sneeze or a sigh. Someone, it seemed, hadn't got the memo.

Emma stared at her husband-to-be in alarmed confusion as an electric, expectant silence tautened the near-empty sanctuary and people in the congregation started turning their heads, craning their necks to catch a glimpse of the mystery speaker. Her groom was looking just as surprised as she was, his forehead crinkled as his uncertain gaze swept the church for the unknown speaker, lost in the shadows in the back.

'You...do?' This from the priest who was marrying them, who also looked confused—there was way too much confusion going on, clearly—peering through the shadowy sanctuary at whoever had spoken with such ringing certainty.

I do was not the answer anyone wanted to the question that had just been given: *'Does anyone have any objections to this marriage? Speak now or for ever hold your peace.'*

No, no one ever wanted to hear someone so much as clear their throat when it came to that particular question. Nobody was supposed to actually *answer* that, Emma thought with a blaze of panic, her mind a blur as she searched the darkened church for the speaker of those damning words. Asking the question was just a matter of form, a relic from a bygone age, even. A second's silence, a silent sigh of relief, a shaky smile, and then they moved on. They said their vows, they left the church, they were married, and everything could go on happily.

'Yes,' the voice from the back of the church called, his tone strident and certain, faintly tinged with an indefinable accent, tickling Emma's consciousness, making her stomach dip.

That voice...

'I most definitely do have objections. One in particular, as it happens.'

The priest was still peering among the pews, where only a handful of guests had gathered—mainly Will's family and a few friends, all of whom had been rather bemused—to put it mildly—at his willingness to marry a woman he'd met only a little over a month ago. They were all looking much more than bemused now, Emma realised as she caught sight of their faces— Will's mother was doing her best impression of a gorgon, stony-faced and sour. She'd never wanted her only son to marry someone she considered a shameless gold-digger, having said so to Emma's face, more than once. Well, so what? There were worse things to be called. Worse things to *be*.

Not that that was what she was. At least, not *exactly*. She was marrying Will for security, it was true, but he knew that and they'd become friends. It would be, she hoped, a good basis for marriage. For a family.

She glanced again at Will's mother and saw her lips twitch in something like satisfaction. Had she arranged this, a way to extricate her son from the so-called siren's seductive claws? Considering Emma had never even kissed Will, who wasn't interested in her that way anyway, being cast in the role of scheming seductress was a little ridiculous. Not that his mother would believe just how chaste their relationship was, especially considering Emma was fourteen weeks pregnant… with another man's child.

A sudden bubble of laughter rose in her throat, and she managed to swallow it down. Bursting into giggles at a moment such as this was definitely not something she wanted to do; the situation was clearly dire enough. She didn't want to make it worse, even if laughing had always been her deliberate, defiant default, her own brand of courage throughout a tumultuous childhood. Laugh instead of cry, show your sense of humour along with your spirit. It had served her well enough in the past, but now…when her life looked about to be derailed, *again*?

'Who are you?' Will called out, uncertain ire flashing in his pale blue eyes. Emma tried to give him an encouraging smile, although the truth was nothing about this situation felt remotely encouraging. Already she could feel her safe and certain future slipping from her fingertips, as it always seemed to.

Just when she'd settled into the latest foster home, got a decent job, managed to save a little bit…every time, something seemed to go wrong. And for someone who had always had to rely on her own wits and not much else, something going wrong could be disastrous. Hopefully that wasn't the case this time, because now she had someone else to consider. Someone tiny and precious and very, very vulnerable.

She straightened, one hand resting on her slight bump as she heard footsteps down the nave of the church, swift and solid.

'Sir?' the priest called, squinting as he tried to catch sight of the figure striding down the nave, each footfall more purposeful than the last, thuds that reverberated through Emma, echoed in her heart. 'What objections can you possibly have to this marriage?'

'What objections?' A shudder ran through her, like an icy finger down her spine, straight through her soul. She *knew* that voice. It was the voice that had haunted her dreams, when she'd woken up in tangled sheets, gasping with a potent mix of desire, hope and grief—a roughened thrum, shot through with a velvety softness, a hint of laughter lurking somewhere deep within the assured rumble, a voice that conjured so many memories, and too many regrets. A voice that had made her smile, even when she hadn't wanted it to.

Hold onto your senses, Emma. Head over heels is definitely not for you, even if you want it to be.

It was a voice she'd never, ever expected to hear again, because its owner was dead.

'My objection,' the owner of that silky, powerful voice continued, coming to the front of the church, a shaft of sunlight from the stained glass above gilding his dark hair in gold, 'is that the bride is already married. To me.'

Nico Santini turned blazing green eyes towards Emma, who felt as if she'd turned to stone. Or maybe ice, because, looking at the freezing fury in her husband's eyes, she suddenly felt very, very cold. Another shiver went through her, and she dropped her bouquet, white rose petals scattering across the stone floor of the church, releasing their heavy scent, making nausea rise up in her in a tidal wave of realisation as her head swam and her body continued to tremble.

'Nico…' His name came out in a croak. 'How…?' She found her mouth was too dry, her heart pounding too hard, for her to finish that improbable question. *How* could he be here? He was *dead*. Dead! He'd died nearly four months ago, just one week after they'd had a whirlwind romance and wedding, all within the space of a single month. And here she was about to have another one, and… *No.* He couldn't be here. He couldn't be alive. She'd seen the death certificate. They'd had a *funeral.* Or at least a memorial service, as his body had never been found. And then she'd been basically bundled out of the door and onto a plane before she'd barely got out of her mourning dress, as per, apparently, Nico's wishes.

So why was he here, in Los Angeles, looking so thunderous? She'd last seen him in Rome, about to travel to the Maldives, where she'd been so sure he'd been killed in a terrible accident, the engine failing on the small plane he'd hired to take him to one of Santini's world-famous luxury resorts.

A shudder went through her. She couldn't cope with the mix of emotions she felt: surprise, a wary, absurd joy, but most of all a creeping sense of dread. She'd never known this man, she understood that now, never mind that she'd married him in a haze of hope and happiness. She didn't want him here, back from the dead, looking absolutely furious, and understandably so, considering the nature of the situation.

Emma was suddenly, painfully conscious of her pale yellow wedding dress, the bouquet she'd just dropped on the ground, the short veil hiding her hair, and, most of all, the groom next to her, the man she'd been about to marry until her husband had walked through the door. Beyond all that, though, she was tinglingly aware of Nico's thunderous expression as he willed her to look at him, which she wouldn't. Couldn't. Not yet, anyway. What on earth was she meant to do?

'Sir?' the minister demanded, his tone turning slightly querulous.

She had no idea how to handle this situation besides running away, not that she'd get very far in this dress and heels. Nico, *here*. Nico, her *husband*. Except they'd barely known each other and, despite the blaze of happiness she'd felt when he'd taken her in his arms, she'd started to fear he'd been tiring of her anyway, the way everyone else had in her life. Every foster family, every friend, every person who took a kindly interest and then walked away. Her own mother, even. Why should Nico have been any different? His family had certainly seemed to think he hadn't been.

'Emma?' Will's voice was soft, hurt, and she turned to him, saw the wounded look on his face. What could she possibly say to him?

'Will... I... I'm so sorry... I can explain...' Except Emma knew she couldn't, not really. Out of the corner of her eye, she saw his mother swell up like a bullfrog, full of vindication as she turned to the woman on her left, some aunt or other. And then there was Nico... standing there like a dark angel, a determined warrior, fierce and furious and absolutely certain.

Her husband...back from the dead.

'Emma, what's going on?' Will asked, his voice rising a little. 'Who is this guy? Are you actually married to him?'

'I told you about Nico...' Emma began, in a whisper.

Will's face flashed with confusion. 'But he *died*—'

'Of course, she knows me,' Nico cut him off, his voice vibrating with icy contempt. 'And yes, she is married to me. I am her husband.' His gaze swung from Will back to Emma, pinning her in place. Eyes as green as moss, and she'd seen them soft with desire, smiling down at her before he'd lowered his lips towards hers for a long and lingering kiss. Now those eyes looked like chips of emerald, glinting hard and cold. Well, there was no love lost on her side, either, all things considered. There had been no love at all, because she hadn't known him. He hadn't known her. No matter what she'd tried to let herself believe.

'Emma?' Will said again. The priest cleared his

throat. Nico stared at her, his cold gaze not wavering. This was hideous. Hideous and unimaginable and really rather terrifying, because Nico wasn't playing the besotted lover now. He looked as if he hated her, and maybe he did. Maybe he had before he left for the Maldives, or almost.

'Nico was already tiring of you, Emma. He said as much to me. The sooner you leave, the better.'

After a lifetime of being passed like a parcel, she knew when it was time to get out. When she wasn't wanted. She'd learned to read the signs—the flash of impatience in the eyes, the tightening of the lips, the weighted pauses and significant looks. And of course sometimes she didn't need to read them; they were spelled out in blazing big lights.

'Adopt Emma? Absolutely not.'

Her foster mother's voice, laced with incredulity, echoed painfully through her all these years later. Yes, Emma knew what rejection looked like, felt like, and so she hadn't waited around to face it again.

Now she opened her mouth. Closed it. Will let out a soft sound of distress, and the look of scorn on her husband's face was mixed with an arrogant, blazing satisfaction. He was clearly in control here, calling the shots just as he always had before. As happy as she'd let herself be, Emma had been under no illusions about who had had the control in their short-lived relationship—Nico. Always Nico.

He was the one who had set the parameters of their affair. *'A few weeks in New York, yes, I'll fly you to Rome, it will end when I say it does.'*

And then, to her shock, he'd asked her to marry

him, and even though she should have known better, she'd agreed. She'd wanted the fairy tale, no matter how brief it turned out to be. It was no surprise at all that Nico had come to regret his uncharacteristically impulsive decision.

'I...' she began, and then found she couldn't go on. In addition to already feeling icy, incredulous and yes, terrified, she was also starting to feel dizzy. Very dizzy, because even as she stared at Nico standing there like an avenging angel her vision was starting to tunnel and she had a strange metallic taste in her mouth.

'Yes, Emma?' Nico drawled coldly.

'I...' She couldn't see to get past that one word. A whisper ran through the congregation like a lit fuse. The world was blacking at its edges, as if she were looking through a telescope, and Will was still gazing at her with a puppyish mixture of hurt and concern. She wasn't brave enough to look at Nico again.

Once more Emma tried to speak. No words came out. There were spots dancing in front of her eyes, and the sight of Nico was becoming smaller and smaller, like a pinpoint at the centre of her eye, shrinking into the distance. If only he would go away completely...

'Emma—' Will said, stepping towards her, but it was too late.

The last thing she saw before she crumpled to the floor was Nico's incredulous fury emblazoned on every taut line of his beautiful face.

Well, that certainly was one way for his errant wife to weasel out of a situation. Nico tamped down on his fury as he stepped forward to Emma's crumpled form. Her erstwhile groom was looking at her in dismay, fluttering his hands uselessly. What a waste of space, stuffed in a suit. He needed to be got rid of immediately, along with all these rubbernecking guests.

'Clear the way,' Nico commanded as he bent to pick up his wife. She smelled of the roses from her fallen bouquet along with the scent that was uniquely her, a scent he remembered, that he'd breathed in deeply. He'd once asked her what perfume it was, and she'd laughed, a gurgle of pure enjoyment.

'Just soap,' she'd told him, her golden eyes dancing, sparkling like bits of amber. 'Eau de Dollar Store.'

He'd laughed back and snatched her up in his arms, breathed in the sweet, soapy scent of her hair, revelling in her, in *them*. What a fool he'd been. What a naïve, deluded fool.

'Sir—' the groom began, and Nico silenced him with a single look, swift and blazing.

'Your part in this farce is over,' he told the man flatly. 'Emma Dunnett—Emma *Santini*—is my wife. I'll take over from here. You can see yourself out, along with all your guests. As quickly as possible, if you please.'

He drew Emma, lolling lifelessly in his arms, against his chest. She was light, her body lithe and slender, maybe even more than he remembered. Her golden-brown hair was wreathed in roses with a short veil, and she wore a simple ankle-length shift dress of pale yellow. At least she hadn't worn wedding white, he thought sardonically.

How could she have betrayed him like this?

And yet, why should he be surprised? He'd had betrayal in his life before, a string of deceptions that were still painful to acknowledge. His mother's affair, his father's remoteness, all based on the lie of who he was—and who he wasn't. If the people he'd loved most in the world had deceived him so utterly, another treacherous act should hardly shock him… and yet from her.

From her.

The priest, having sprung into motion, gestured for Nico to head to a small room off the sanctuary of the church. Nico deposited Emma on a small, worn sofa and stepped back.

'Sir,' the priest stammered, 'this is highly irregular…'

'We'll be out of your way in a few minutes,' Nico assured him, 'after my wife has regained her senses. Could you please leave Emma's things outside the door for my driver to retrieve?'

He had a car waiting outside, and no interest or intention in staying here for a single second longer than necessary.

'Please, if you could leave us alone,' he commanded, and with an unhappy look the priest scurried away. Nico heard the murmur of voices and click of heels before the door closed, and he knew the guests were leaving. Good.

As he gazed down at the supine form of his wife, he hoped, belatedly, that she hadn't injured herself, but then acknowledged that, despite her fall, Emma was clearly someone who always landed on her feet. She'd demonstrated that admirably today.

Her eyes fluttered open, and she caught sight of him—a gleam of awareness brightening her golden irises before her lids drifted shut again.

Lord help him, but she was beautiful. More beautiful than he'd even remembered. And he'd spent *months* remembering—months in a hospital bed, trying to remember his own name, her face feeling like the only thing his mind hadn't let him forget.

And that face was before him right now—heart-shaped and pale, her faintly snub nose scattered with golden freckles, her pink lips slightly parted. Her chest rose and fell in pants that were too agitated to be the deep and even breathing of someone rendered unconscious.

'Open your eyes, Emma,' Nico commanded flatly. 'I know you're awake.'

If anything her lids scrunched even more tightly shut. Nico let out a huff that would have been laughter if he'd been remotely amused. He wasn't, because he was too angry for that. And he was angry because that felt so much better than being hurt.

Just a little over three months he'd been gone. Three *months*.

'Emma.'

A breath shuddered out of her as she kept her eyes resolutely closed. 'I don't feel like opening them,' she confessed in a croaky whisper.

'Because you want me to just go away,' Nico surmised in a hard voice. 'I'm not surprised.'

Finally Emma cracked open a single eye, to gaze at him uncertainly. 'Aren't you?'

'No, why should I be, considering how quickly you

were able to forget me?' he replied coolly. 'Two weddings in the space of three months has to be a record for just about anyone.'

'Three and a half months,' she corrected weakly, and this time Nico did let out a huff of laughter—hard, humourless laughter, because she was certainly showing her true colours now. How could he have ever been so deceived? Because he'd let himself, he knew. Because, after the revelation of his own birth, he'd wanted to belong to someone. Well, lesson learned. Abundantly. Don't go looking for love. Don't even believe it exists, because he had yet to see it in his own life, from his own father.

'I stand corrected,' he told her. 'Three and a half months from one wedding to the next...those two weeks make *all* the difference, clearly.'

She opened both eyes this time as she regarded him with a weary sort of apprehension. 'How is it that you are alive?'

'You sound so pleased that I am.' She didn't reply and he forced himself to continue, not to dwell on the truth that was staring him so bleakly in the face. She'd never cared about him at all. He'd just been a meal ticket, as his cousin Antonio had told him, right from the beginning, incredulous that he'd been so foolhardy as to marry a woman after an acquaintance of a mere three weeks. Nico had scoffed at his cousin, determined to believe that he was acting only out of spite and jealousy; their relationship had become increasingly strained since his father's revelations, with Antonio embittered at not being handed the reins of Santini Enterprises.

And yet he, usually so pragmatic and resolute, had let himself, in a rare moment of weakness, be deluded by the most absurd fantasy. Well, no longer. Not for one second more. 'I'm alive,' he told her, 'because I survived the plane crash. Obviously.'

She shook her head slowly, eyes wide as she stared at him in dismay. Clearly she didn't relish the idea of living together as husband and wife again. Well, it wasn't all appealing to him either, but he'd be damned if he'd let her commit bigamy by marrying another man.

'But where have you been for the last three months?' she asked, her voice sounding thin and papery. She was lying on the sofa like some sort of Snow White, her hair spread about the cushion, the circlet of roses having been knocked askew. Her figure was elegant and lithe, reminding Nico of how he'd explored every inch of that body, every intriguing dip and lush curve, how he'd made them his own.

He clenched his hands into fists to keep from reaching for her, even now. 'Three and a half months, you mean,' he reminded her in a voice like a blade, cutting and quick. 'After the plane crashed into the Indian Ocean, I was rescued by a fishing boat, and then I was in a cottage hospital on a nearby island. After that I was transferred to a rehabilitation centre in Jakarta, before I returned to Rome last week. Any other questions?'

'Why didn't you let me know you were alive?' This came out more stridently, a golden blaze in her eyes that reminded him of why he'd fallen in love with her, or at least thought he had. That spirit, that humour, the sparkle in her eye, the quirk of her lip. It had lightened something inside him, something that had desperately needed lightening, but of course it had all been false, a tissue of carefully constructed lies, because he'd never known her at all, not truly. That reality was staring him smack in the face right now.

'Because first I was in a coma,' he explained flatly, 'and then I couldn't remember my own name. I had no identification, no way of anyone knowing who I was. That had been destroyed in the crash.' His voice pulsed with a pain that he did his best to hide. Those months had been torturous in their own way, and yet in the midst of all the pain and uncertainty, he'd remembered her. He almost wished now that he hadn't.

Emma's golden eyes widened as she scooted up on the sofa. 'You were in a *coma*?'

'It's a little late to sound concerned.'

Her mouth dropped open, eyes flashing. 'Nico, you can't blame me for not knowing—'

'I can,' he informed her in a voice of silky, suppressed rage, 'blame you for marrying the next man who offered. I assume he was the next man?' He jerked his head towards the door to the sanctuary, which he sincerely hoped was now empty of guests—and groom. 'Not a very impressive specimen, all told. Really, you could have done better.'

'Don't insult Will,' she replied with quiet, dignified resignation. 'Or blame him. He's done nothing to you.'

True, but Nico felt a scorching flash of fury all the same. 'No,' he agreed when he trusted his tone to be pleasant. 'I don't blame him. Quite the contrary, my dear.' He bared his teeth in the semblance of a smile as he took a step closer to her, watched her shrink against the cushions of faded velvet. Was she pretending to be afraid of him, to add to the drama, appeal to some sort of sympathy? Damsel in distress was a role she knew how to play to the hilt, but it wouldn't work this time. Far from it. 'I don't blame your groom,' he told her with succinct, acid sweetness. 'I blame you.'

CHAPTER TWO

EMMA GAZED AT the fury simmering in her husband's eyes and felt everything in her shrink. She supposed she should expect him to be angry, but that sneering derision twisting his lips made her want to curl up in a ball, close her eyes again, and pretend he wasn't here. This was such a *mess*.

Their marriage had been a mistake. She was pretty sure Nico had already been coming to that conclusion, even if he liked to bask in his self-righteous rage now. Yes, she *had* been about to marry another man, mere months after she'd married him. And yes, he had been declared dead, but such a trifling consideration wouldn't bother Nico. He'd always seemed to her a man who understood right and wrong, saw it in stark, certain terms—unlike her, who'd had to bend the truth more than once just to survive. Who had learned not to trust in happily-ever-afters, even if she'd dared, ever so briefly, to wonder if she could have one with Nico.

Now Emma knew that their marriage never would have lasted past the honeymoon stage, and, with another person to consider, she wasn't about to jump into that shark tank again. Looking at Nico's furious expression, she doubted he wanted her to, either. So why was he here?

'Emma?' he prompted silkily. 'Care to make any explanation as to why you wanted to enter into matrimony with another man so soon after you had done so with me?'

'Because I needed to,' Emma replied bluntly. 'Something you could never understand.' She folded her arms and looked away, telling herself she could deal with his anger, because the truth was she preferred it. If he stayed angry, she wouldn't remember how kind he'd once been. How considerate and tender, in a way that had just begun to chip away at the carefully constructed walls she'd built around her heart, brick by necessary brick.

Don't trust anyone. Don't let people in. Definitely don't start to care, because then you'll get hurt. You'll be rejected by the people you'd come to trust, which hurts so much more.

Well, fortunately she hadn't started to care. Much. He'd died—or she'd thought he had—before her defences had been truly breached, and in the three and a half months since then she'd had plenty of time—and reason—to build them up again. He was angry? Well, so was she. His family had treated her abominably, and she'd had no reason to think Nico wouldn't have gone along with it, had he been alive. She had decided a long time ago that she would never stay somewhere she wasn't wanted, and Nico certainly didn't look as though he wanted her now.

But he doesn't know about the baby.

And how on earth was she supposed to tell him,

when he was already so furious with her? The last thing she wanted was for Nico Santini to order her life around, all while in a self-righteous rage. She didn't deserve that, and her baby didn't, either.

'You needed to,' Nico repeated, his voice positively dripping with sarcasm. 'Really.' He towered above her, arms folded, biceps rippling, a vengeful god in a three-piece suit. Three months in a coma or hospital or wherever had not diminished his hotness one bit, Emma acknowledged sourly. It would have helped if it had. Why couldn't he look a little…anaemic? Injured, at least? The only sign that he'd been in a crash at all was a scar by his eyebrow, and in fact that livid little line just added to his sexiness, drat the man. The close-cropped ink-dark hair and vivid green eyes didn't help, either, along with the body that, despite being in a hospital bed for several months, looked every bit as powerfully muscular as it ever had. Everything about Nico Santini was potently virile, intoxicatingly male. And right now she really wished it weren't.

'Yes, really,' she replied with a shrug, as if it were a matter of indifference, as if her heart wasn't threatening to jackhammer through her chest. Nico would never understand what it was like to need something— security, safety, a roof over your head. He would never believe that she'd had a genuine friendship with Will, that she hadn't been taking him for a ride. She certainly wasn't about to explain any of it to him, only to be scoffed at. 'You were dead, Nico, or so I thought. I don't have to offer excuses, and you have no right to be angry.'

'No right!' He looked outraged, and a sudden laugh

rose in her throat like a bubble. Thankfully she swallowed it down. She did not want to incite his rage any more than she already had.

'No right,' she repeated. 'We'd only been married a week. We barely knew each other. How long did you expect me to play the grieving widow?'

'Longer than you did, clearly,' he bit out, the skin around his mouth turning white before he swung away from her.

Emma was under no illusions that he was hurt by what she'd done. He hadn't loved her, after all. She'd always known that, deep down. Nico might have played the attentive lover for a while, but it had never been real. Their relationship had never been tested, had never had a chance to see if it would endure. And when he'd died—or at least she'd thought he had—his true colours had been revealed by his family.

No, he was angry because of his pride, she supposed. He'd always made it clear he would be the one who decided when their relationship ended. Well, she had been the one to end it, but then he'd been *dead*.

'So you have no excuses,' Nico stated flatly as he turned around, his expression now forbidding. 'Nothing to exonerate yourself.'

'I don't need to exonerate myself, and I really don't know what you expect me to say.' Emma glared up at him as she folded her arms, mainly to hide her very small bump, because she was pretty sure he didn't realise she was pregnant—with his child. And when he realised that…well, she had no idea what he might do. She doubted he wanted to continue their marriage, all things considered, but she would die before she let him take her child away from her, the only family she'd ever had. She had no intention of revealing anything more than she had to, not until she knew what Nico wanted. Not until she could trust him with the truth.

Yet looking at those glinting green eyes narrowed in anger, she still remembered—painfully, shamefully—how soft and mossy they'd seemed after she'd first met him, how he'd looked at her with something almost like love. Of course, it hadn't really been love, not even close. She knew that, of course she did, but still, it had felt...well, as close to love as she'd ever known, maybe, which was pretty pathetic, she acknowledged now, especially since Nico had made it clear at the start that he didn't love her.

She'd been fine with that, had accepted it, as she'd accepted it for her whole life. Something about her, she suspected, had always been fundamentally unlovable, if the foster families she'd cycled through were anything to go by. Whether it was indifference, weary kindness, or outright cruelty, they'd all abandoned her in the end. But now...now she had to think differently, because now she had to watch out for someone else, as well. Someone infinitely important. Someone whose well-being mattered far, far more than her own.

She'd been a waitress at a small Italian bistro in New York when she'd met Nico just five months ago, the kind of hole-in-the-wall place that billionaires weren't supposed to frequent, and yet Nico had. He had a table in the window, his paperwork spread out while he sipped a glass of Chianti; and Emma walked by him, transfixed by the blade-like precision of his cheekbones, the fullness of his lips, the breadth of his shoulders, the expensive fabric of his shirt stretching tautly across them as he studied the papers before him with a remarkable and focussed intensity.

He was utterly unaware of her, of course—that was, until she breathed in the spicy scent of his cologne and, stupidly overwhelmed by its heady fragrance assaulting her senses, she tripped over her own feet and managed to dump an entire plate of spaghetti and meatballs right into his lap.

He jumped up, appalled and furious, accidentally knocking his glass of wine over his papers in the process. He snatched the glass to turn it upright, but of course it was too late. He was covered in sauce and his papers were covered in wine. Total disaster.

And Emma, because it was all so awful, and she was pretty sure she was going to get fired for causing it, laughed. It was her default, her defence mechanism, a way to not let herself be hurt by the casual cruelty, or, sometimes even worse, pitying kindness she'd encountered throughout her life. And, face it, a gorgeous man with a crotch full of spaghetti *was* funny. Sort of.

A horrified giggle escaped her in a bubble of sound, and he swung his infuriated and incredulous gaze towards her before she clapped her hand over her mouth. Now was not the time to laugh, she told herself severely, not when this incredibly handsome and obviously powerful man had just had his dinner, his paperwork and his suit all ruined—by her. And she knew how powerful people liked to blame their underlings for just about everything. Not that she'd met anyone remotely as powerful and magnetic as the man in front of her, spaghetti and all.

'I'm so sorry,' she said, trying for a deeply contrite tone, even as another giggle escaped through her fingers.

Nico stared at her for an endless moment, and for the first time she got the full effect of his eyes—like emerald lasers—as well as his beauty. *Sculpted* was the word that came to mind, except that conjured an image of statues of white marble, lifeless and cold. Nico was very much alive, pulsing with disbelief and anger, and yes, beauty. He really was the most beautiful man. His eyelashes, Emma noted with a distant numbness, were ridiculously long. And curly. What kind of man had lashes like that and still looked formidably, potently male? Because he certainly did.

'Are you actually laughing?' he demanded, his voice a low rasp, lightly accented, and she forced her mind away from his eyelashes and shook her head, her hand still pressed to her mouth.

'No...' she managed, not all that convincingly.

Nico didn't have time to reply, because the manager and owner of the restaurant, Tony, swept down upon them, full of apologies—and fury for Emma.

'Signor Santini, I am so sorry! I cannot believe this has happened! This stupid, clumsy girl, she will be fired! Immediately.' Tony, who had been all paternal friendliness to Emma before now, glared at her. 'Get your things. You will leave at once.'

'It was an accident...' Emma whispered, rather feebly, because already she knew there was no point. She supposed she deserved to be fired, after such a mishap, and yet it still stung—and scared her. Jobs weren't easy to get without a reference, and she was living paycheque to paycheque as it was. She had maybe ten bucks in her purse and nothing to eat. She watched as Nico picked a strand of spaghetti from his trousers, and, with a rather wryly self-deprecating look, deposited it on the table.

'I'll go,' she told Tony, 'but you still owe me a week's wages.'

'The impertinence!' her boss huffed, flapping his hands at her. 'A week's wages, when you have insulted my best customer! Away with you.'

Even though she trembled inside, Emma forced herself to stand her ground. 'I'm very sorry about what happened,' she replied steadily, trying not to let a tell-tale tremor creep into her voice, 'but I have worked here all week and I am owed that money.' And she needed it. Desperately.

'Your wages,' Tony informed her coldly, 'will go towards reimbursing Signor Santini for his suit.'

'That won't be necessary,' Nico informed the ruffled restaurateur. He turned to Emma, his look wry but also knowingly magnanimous, as if he were being so very generous with this concession. 'But I imagine your wages might just about cover the dry-cleaning bill.'

What an absolute gentleman, Emma thought sarcastically, *being so generous*.

She knew his suit had probably cost hundreds, if not thousands, of dollars, and there was no way she could pay for it—or even the dry-cleaning. Both were well within his budget, though. *He* wasn't wondering how he'd pay the rent this week, or where his next meal was coming from. No one who hadn't lived on that knife edge could possibly understand how it felt, balancing precariously, always in danger of life slicing you right open.

'Fine,' she snapped out, because she had no choice and, even in her most desperate moments, she'd never let herself beg. Not even to a man as potently handsome as this. While Tony fumed and Signor Santini stared at her in bemusement, clearly having expected her to fall about in gratitude, she turned on her heel and stalked away. Her fingers trembled as she undid her apron strings, flung it on the pile of dirty laundry in the kitchen. One of the chefs gave her a sympathetic look.

'Tough one, Em.'

'Yeah.' She tilted her chin, gave him a smile of pure bravado. She might deserve it, but she didn't particularly want anyone's pity. She'd stood on her own two feet for too long to go courting that. She took her coat and left the bistro without a backward glance, even though she had no destination in mind. She owed the week's rent on the shabby room she rented in Hell's Kitchen, and now she didn't have it. She could grab her stuff, at least, but she knew her landlord, a guy with a beer belly and a wandering eye, would not allow her to sleep there with the rent unpaid. Not unless she offered him some *favours*, which she had no intention of doing.

So what would it be? A homeless shelter? Sleeping on the street? Oh, the options were *so* attractive. She didn't really have any friends in this city, not yet anyway. She'd only been here for a couple of months, try-ing to figure out her next move, as always, and barely one step ahead. A sigh escaped her as she continued to put one foot in front of the other, yet with no idea where she would go.

She was halfway down the street when Signor San-tini caught up with her.

'Excuse me—miss?'

She turned to him, eyes narrowed in suspicion. Did he want her to pay for his suit, after all? As if she could. Or was he angling for something else, the way her landlord was? Although, Emma acknowledged, that might be flattering herself rather a bit too much.

'It occurred to me that you might have been treated a bit unfairly,' he told her quietly, surprising her, be-cause *that* she really hadn't expected. 'It was an ac-cident, after all.'

'Might have?' Emma repeated, with spirit, before she could control her tongue. 'A *bit*?' He raised his eyebrows and her momentary courage immediately deserted her. Here he was apologising and she still couldn't keep from coming out swinging. It tended to be her default, along with the laughter. Ways to fight when you had no other weapons. 'It *was* an accident, and I really am sorry,' she told him, because she sup-posed he deserved that much, no matter the man's ar-rogance. 'I really do hope your suit's not ruined and those papers weren't too, uh, important.'

'They were a crucial contract,' he replied, smiling a little, 'that has to be signed today.'

'Oh.' What was she supposed to say to that?

'Fortunately, I was thinking I needed a little more

time to consider the matter, and now I have it.' He raised his eyebrows again, a smile lurking about his mouth, revealing a dimple. Suddenly this man—this incredibly handsome, powerful, glorious-looking man—seemed somewhat approachable. Kind, even. And Emma's deliberately hardened heart thawed the tiniest little bit.

That was when she should have turned around and walked away, Emma reflected as she gazed up at Nico standing above her now, filled with self-righteous fury. She should have run as fast as she could in the opposite direction, knowing it was always better to guard her heart and stay safe. Instead he'd asked her out to dinner, and she'd said yes, because she'd been hungry and she'd had nowhere to go, and also because he'd intrigued her, this man with so much power, and yet who had kind eyes and a dimple. That dinner had turned into an evening, into a weekend, into an affair she'd expected to end at any moment, when Nico said it would.

Instead, three weeks later, they'd been married.

What had he *expected* her to say?

Nico stared at Emma in incredulity, irritated beyond measure that his wife could be so utterly unrepentant. There was not a flicker of guilt in those golden eyes, although she did, he acknowledged, look tired. And pale—too pale. Now that he was looking at her properly, he realised how completely exhausted she seemed, with violet shadows under her eyes, and a drawn look about her mouth. Despite the curves he'd noticed earlier, there was a gauntness to her face and arms that alarmed him. This was not the Emma he remembered, the one he'd left in their marital bed, smiling sleepily up at him as he'd wound a tendril of curling golden-brown hair around one finger and drawn her towards him for one last kiss.

'I'll be back in a couple of days,' he'd told her, and she'd fallen back against the pillows, her heart-shaped face framed by navy satin, a smile of pure satisfaction curving her lips.

They'd spent the last hour in bed, and a very pleasant hour it had been. Although pleasant didn't even touch what he'd found with her—powerful was a more accurate word, explosive even better. When he touched Emma, his head reeled and his senses spun and his body ached. Their chemistry had shocked, thrilled and frightened him all at once, because he'd never, ever experienced it with anyone else. He'd never been in love, not even close, and he'd wondered if it was love with Emma. He'd almost wanted it to be, fool that he was. Good thing he'd come to his senses before it was too late, but their explosive chemistry was why he was reluctant to touch her now. He needed to keep his focus.

'So you have no explanation to offer,' he stated coldly, 'as to why you were willing to marry another man just three months—'

'Three and a half,' she reminded him with that cheeky smile he remembered from when they'd met. It was the same smile she'd given him right after she'd dumped a plate of spaghetti in his lap and then started to laugh—had that all been planned, an admittedly unorthodox way to arrange a meeting? How could she have possibly known how charmed he would have been by her honesty, her artlessness? When so much of his life had turned to lies, the family he'd considered his bedrock crumbling around him, he'd appreciated her unvarnished candour, her willingness to laugh at life, to take it as it came, unlike him, with the familial duty that had always weighed heavily on his shoulders, never more so when he'd discovered the deception at its base.

Too bad he'd been utterly wrong about it all. Ridiculously naïve, which stung even more, because he was smarter than that. He would never be so naïve again.

'Three and half,' he agreed tersely. 'Thank you so much for pointing that out.'

'You're welcome.'

Nico gritted his teeth, amazed and infuriated by her seeming insouciance. Even lying there, looking exhausted, she still had the same impish spirit that had first attracted him to her. But now was surely not the time to be cracking jokes. He wanted her humble, contrite, *begging* him to take her back, despite her betrayal. It would have gone some way to dampening down his anger.

'I would have thought,' he said through his teeth, 'that you might be a bit more regretful, all things considered.'

'I'm not sure why you would think that,' Emma returned, eyes flashing. 'You were declared dead. I was free to marry.'

'In indecent haste—'

'Says who?'

Nico stared at her, amazed at how she was continually coming up swinging—almost as if she were angry

at him, or perhaps simply she didn't care at all. Yet
something about it, he realised, didn't make sense, not
if she was what Antonio had told him she was, what
she'd shown herself to be—a shameless gold-digger
only interested in cold, hard cash.

'She had her hand out before I'd even written the
cheque,' had been his exact words. 'And she couldn't
leave fast enough, Nico.'

Even with the strain that had developed between
him and his cousin in recent months, Nico had believed
him, and, in any case, Emma marrying the next man
who offered paid proof to his cousin's words. Not that
he should have been surprised. He'd married Emma
in a moment of weakness; he'd only been intending
an affair when his passion would spend itself and then
they'd both go their separate ways, satisfied. It should
have happened that way, but instead, reeling from the
news he'd been given, he'd chosen to marry her, a
woman unlike any other he'd encountered—and it was
something he'd obviously had cause to regret. The
three months' rehabilitation, where he'd clung to hazy
memories and half-hoped-for dreams had put her on
a pedestal. Well, she'd been knocked right off it now.

But he still couldn't quite believe her gall at seeming so angry at him. Why wasn't she, the shameless
gold-digger she was meant to be, on her hands and
knees, begging to come back? You didn't annoy the
golden goose when it had made an unexpected reappearance, after all. You thanked your lucky stars and
did your best to seem contrite and humble so you could
keep gathering all those lovely eggs.

Emma was definitely *not* doing that. Why not? Why

was she showing her true colours so unabashedly? Was it because he'd caught her in the act, about to marry some other sop? Or was something else going on, something he didn't know about, didn't understand?

'Perhaps you have not considered the implications of my survival,' he remarked coolly. 'I am not dead, and so you are, in fact, still legally married to me.'

The sudden vulnerable look in her eyes as she shrank back against the sofa made him realise, uncomfortably, that he didn't actually *want* her cowering or begging, although what he *did* want still remained to be seen.

'I assumed,' Emma said after a moment, her voice coming out in something close to a croak, 'that you wouldn't wish to be married to me any longer, all things considered.'

'All things considered? What things would those be, Emma?'

She looked away, her hands still folded across her middle. 'We only knew each other a couple of weeks, Nico. They were amazing weeks, it was true, but... I always expected you to regret our marriage.' She paused, biting her lip. 'If you hadn't been in that crash...'

She trailed off and he took a step towards her. 'If I hadn't been in that crash...?' he prompted softly.

Emma shrugged, still not looking at him. 'We would have divorced eventually, don't you think? Our marriage was clearly a mistake.'

'I can certainly see that now.' Although her saying it so plainly still stung, even as he acknowledged there was some truth in her words. They'd married in haste, as virtual strangers. Perhaps he would have regretted it.

'Why did you agree, then, just out of curiosity?'

She turned back to him, her eyes sparking golden defiance. 'Because...because I wanted to be happy, if only for a little while, and it was the best offer I'd had in a long time,' she told him bluntly, lifting her chin a little. 'Something else you could never understand.'

So she really was unabashed about it, Nico acknowledged dispassionately. Well, fine. At least he knew now, for certain.

'Now we know where we stand,' he told her, his smile a mere stretching of his lips. 'Considering the nature of our situation, I'm sure an annulment can be arranged, and, if not, then a divorce.' The words fell heavily from him; no matter what he felt right now, or in what haste he'd married this woman, he'd still intended to take his vows seriously. Unlike Emma.

Her face paled and something almost, almost like hurt flashed in her eyes before her chin tilted that little bit higher. 'If that's what you want.'

'Isn't it what you want?' he challenged mockingly. 'You're hardly tripping over yourself to win me back, Emma. Really, considering the state of my portfolio, I would have expected a *slightly* warmer welcome. After all, I have a feeling my bank balance is decidedly more impressive than the one of the guy out there you were willing to give yourself to.' His stomach cramped as he briefly imagined such an unsavoury scene. 'What was his name? Will something?'

'Will Trent,' she said quietly.

'Was he really the best you could find?' He shook

his head in a parody of disappointment. 'At least you're not pretending to be the woebegone widow. I suppose you're pragmatic enough to realise it would be too hard to pull off.' Perhaps that was why she seemed so reluctant; she knew she'd already been rumbled. 'All in all,' he finished, 'this is probably the better play. Kudos for thinking of it.'

She closed her eyes as she shook her head, her face pale. 'This isn't a *play*.'

'No, I suppose not,' he acknowledged, unable to keep from jeering, 'considering you don't have an angle left, do you? No way to win me back. Too bad.'

'I don't want to win you back,' she flashed, her eyes opening, the anger in their depths jolting him. 'Why would I?'

The stark honesty he saw in her expression felt like a fist to his solar plexus. Clearly his bank balance wasn't enough of a draw, a fact that shouldn't have hurt, of course not, and yet somehow still did. 'Then at least we're in agreement,' he told her. 'Because I don't want you back, either.'

Emma let out a sound that Nico suspected was meant to be a laugh but came out more like a sob. 'Why did you even come here, Nico?'

'I suppose I needed to see for myself.' He hadn't wanted to believe his cousin. Hadn't wanted to believe Emma wasn't what she'd seemed, what he'd made her into during his three months' rehabilitation.

'Well, now you have,' she said wearily, and he gave one, terse nod.

'Now I have.' And yet he was, bizarrely, still reluctant to simply walk out on her. He could arrange an annulment or even a divorce without the need to see her again; why wasn't he doing just that? Why was he standing here, somehow unwilling even now to let her go? Emma, he acknowledged, had got right under his skin. Wormed her way into his—not his heart, no, never that, but his affections. As angry as he was with her—and he *was* angry—he also felt that old tug of desire, that fascination he'd felt when she'd dumped a plate of spaghetti on him and then laughed. He *couldn't* walk away, as much as he wanted to.

'Nico?' she prompted uncertainly. Clearly, she was expecting him to stalk out, just as he'd intended, but he still couldn't make himself do it. They were *married*, and although it had been in haste, he'd taken his vows seriously. Did he want to end their marriage as precipitously as he'd started it?

Did she?

'I'm thinking,' he said slowly, and Emma's eyes narrowed. Then her face went alarmingly pale and she clapped a hand over her mouth. Nico frowned, about to ask her if she was all right, but he wasn't given the chance.

'Sorry,' she gasped out, and then she scrambled off the sofa, rushed to the bathroom adjacent, and wretched loudly and comprehensively into the toilet.

CHAPTER THREE

SHE'D HOPED THE morning sickness was over, Emma reflected as she kneeled in front of the toilet, her cheek resting on the porcelain, her eyes closed. She had just completely voided the contents of her stomach, and Nico had heard it all, heaven help her.

What now?

She felt too worn and weary even to think. Her stomach, even though utterly empty, heaved again, but she managed to swallow it down. She heard his footsteps as he came into the bathroom. She breathed in the smell of his cologne—that same, woodsy scent—and her stomach swirled with nausea even as her heart ached with remembrance. Walking hand in hand, lying in bed, legs tangled together, too afraid and jaded to actually believe someone like her actually got a happily-ever-after, yet hoping still...

Well, obviously she didn't get one, considering the current situation. Except what even was the current situation? What was Nico *thinking* about? And could she really let him walk out of there without knowing about his baby? Yet the alternative felt worse...a loveless marriage with a cold, autocratic man who as good as despised her. Was that what she wanted for her child—the same thing she had, a father who had never really wanted her, who was only there on sufferance?

'You've been sick,' he remarked tonelessly.

'Oh, well done, Sherlock,' Emma returned on a huff of tired laughter. 'A-plus for your deduction skills.' She closed her eyes again, her cheek still pressed against the seat of the toilet, feeling utterly spent.

'Here.' To her surprise Nico crouched down and pressed a square of cloth into her hand—his handkerchief. Briefly she remembered teasing him about always carrying a handkerchief—*'What are you? Mr Darcy or something?'* He'd just smiled and shrugged. She was glad for it now, although she wasn't sure she could take his kindness, even one as small as that.

Slowly she eased up into a sitting position, her back against the wall. She dabbed her lips self-consciously and with a small, wry smile—how she remembered that smile!—Nico leaned over and flushed the toilet.

'Thanks,' she mumbled. 'I'll feel better in a few minutes.'

'Will you?' He cocked an eyebrow. 'Where did that come from? Has the shock of my reappearance made you lose your lunch, or are you suffering from a touch of the flu?'

Emma hesitated, and in that second's damning pause she saw suspicion flash across Nico's features, tightening his mouth. 'Emma?' he prompted silkily while she pressed the handkerchief to her mouth, now simply to stall for time.

She couldn't lie, she realised despondently, not about something as important as this. And yet how could she confess the truth? Considering what she'd seen of Nico today, she didn't know what he'd do. What he was capable of. Would he take her child away from her, the way she'd been taken from her own mother, determined to claim what was his? Or perhaps he'd agree to some 'marriage in name only' arrangement, install her in a flat or house somewhere out of the way... All in all, she supposed she could cope with that, as long as she had her baby, but she had no guarantees that Nico wouldn't cut her out of his life as ruthlessly as if wielding a pair of scissors, considering how angry he was with her. How little he thought he could trust her.

Or, Emma considered hopefully, maybe he'd let her go. Maybe he wouldn't even care about his own child She didn't know him well enough to know, and yet she was afraid to trust him with the truth. She had too much hard experience not to handle things *very* carefully in this regard. Her own childhood had been loveless, miserable. She wanted so much more for her baby.

Yet could she even provide it without Nico? She thought of Will, with both regret and longing. Simple, safe Will, who would have been a good father, who would have given her and her baby a home. Was it wrong to want such basic things? To marry for them?

'Is it the flu, Emma?' Nico asked, his voice a low, velvety thrum, laced with danger.

'Could you help me up, please?' she asked, holding out one hand. 'I'd like a drink of water before I answer your questions.'

'I wouldn't think they would be so very difficult to answer,' he replied, extending a hand. 'Considering it's just the one. "Yes, I've been a bit under the weather" would do it.'

'Well, then, yes, I have been a bit under the weather,' Emma replied tartly, for that much was certainly true. She reached for his hand, jolting at the feel of it—dry and strong, long, tensile fingers clasping over hers as he hauled her to her feet. Remembering how that hand had touched every inch of her body, intimately, tenderly, with possession, making her feel so much pleasure, so much *love*. No, not that. Never that.

Breathless, she stumbled and nearly fell against him, managing to catch herself in the very nick of time. She didn't trust herself when in that much close contact with him, the hard, muscled wall of his chest. Just breathing in the scent of him was enough to have longing course through her, along with the dizziness and nausea, which thankfully was starting to subside.

But Nico still looked suspicious.

'Under the weather,' he repeated neutrally, his gaze tracking her as she made her way back to the sofa. The smell of candle wax and dust peculiar to old churches was adding to her nausea, she decided. She needed fresh air, freedom. And she wanted to stall for time, time to think about how she could handle this, although she had a feeling time wasn't going to help her all that much.

'Could we go somewhere else to have this discussion?' she asked, a bit desperately. 'Somewhere public?' She'd feel safer then, more in control. Maybe then she'd know what to do.

'Of course, my car is waiting,' Nico replied without missing a beat. 'I'll text my driver.' Before Emma could formulate a response, he had thumbed a quick text and then stepped over to her, his hand under her elbow, and was guiding her towards the door.

'I don't want to go in your car,' she protested help-lessly, for he was propelling her inexorably towards the church doors, so she had no choice but to walk with him. The sanctuary was abandoned, the only evidence that a wedding had been meant to take place were a few white rose petals still scattered across the floor, now curling and brown.

'Where else would you go?' Nico replied. 'Besides, you said you wanted a drink of water, and you look like you need a good meal. We'll go somewhere quiet and private to eat, drink.' He let a weighty pause settle between them. 'And talk.'

Oh, yes, *talk*. And what was she supposed to say? She didn't think she could actually keep the truth of his own child from him, Emma realised afresh, as much as that might be the wise thing to do, consid-ering how hostile he was being. It felt smart, but it didn't feel right.

They'd stepped out of the church into a balmy Cali-fornia evening, the sky a stream of pink and lavender, the air holding the salt-tinged scent of the sea along with the choking smell of LA's usual car pollution. An SUV with blacked-out windows was idling by the kerb. A blank-faced chauffeur emerged from the driver's seat and opened the door for them to climb in the back.

As Nico continued to propel her towards the car, Emma finally balked. 'You can't frogmarch me in there,' she declared, digging her heels—all three inches of them—into the pavement. Typical of him to take total control.

Nico's breath came out in a quick, irritated rush. 'I'm not *frogmarching* you anywhere. I'm taking you to a restaurant in my car, so we can talk in a civilised manner.'

'What is there to talk about?' Emma challenged. She heard the desperation in her voice, and she knew Nico heard it, as well.

'Plenty, it seems,' he said grimly, and, without further ado, he took her elbow again and once more propelled her towards the car.

'If that wasn't frogmarching,' Emma tossed at him as she scrambled across the seat, 'I don't know what was.'

Nico let out a huff of hard laughter. 'You haven't lost your spirit, I see,' he said as the driver closed the door. Emma couldn't tell if it was a compliment.

She still amused him, Nico acknowledged reluctantly as Emma scooted as far away from him as she could, arms folded as she avoided his gaze, looking determinedly out of the window. Amused and aggravated him in equal measure, but still. He was, rather perversely, glad that she hadn't lost her spirit, that cheekiness that had made him laugh, what felt like a million years ago but was, in fact, only three months.

Three and a *half* months. He wasn't about to forget that. And why should he think she had lost such a quality, simply because he'd lost his? She'd been cartwheeling through life, it seemed, from one husband to another, while he had been struggling to hold onto his memories, and then regretting it when he did...

Nico pushed such useless thoughts away. As much as he regretted the past, he had to think of the future now, and how he was going to handle his errant wife, and he still didn't have a good answer to that, no matter what he'd suggested to her earlier in a fit of pique.

He'd come to Los Angeles on something between a vendetta and a whim, needing to see her for himself. He hadn't wanted to believe his cousin, Antonio, when he'd told her Emma had moved on immediately after the memorial service, had left for California while still wearing her widow's black. When Antonio had admitted that he'd kept tabs on her and knew she was seeing someone else, Nico had been shocked—and devastated, trying to hide the depth of his feeling from the rather cool gaze of his cousin.

'I'm sorry, Nico,' he'd said, with the slightest of grimaces. 'But at least now you know what she's really like. A ruthless schemer, after your money, just as I'd said. I'm glad her true colours were revealed before too much time had passed. After all, it hardly befits the CEO of Santini Enterprises to have such a...questionable wife.'

And Antonio would rather he was CEO himself, Nico suspected. In any case, time *had* passed, three whole months where he'd stupidly lived for her memory, pinned all his hopes on their joyful reunion. What a joke. He hadn't been able to make himself reply to his cousin's scathing assessment of Emma, but he'd got on the next plane to LA, to see her for himself.

And because she was his *wife*, and he wasn't about to let her marry someone else.

But did he still want to be married to her himself? Live out their years together? Divorce didn't sit well with him, but neither did marriage, not when he knew what she was really like. Although, he told himself, perhaps that was a plus. No dishonesty, no prevarications...just honest desire. Because she still desired him, that much he knew. He'd felt the tremble in her slender body as he'd caught her in his arms. Felt the roar of response in himself. That kind of physical attraction wasn't, he reflected, to be dismissed out of hand. Maybe it was actually better this way...no love lost, after all. And he'd never meant to love her, anyway, because after all the deceptions of his childhood he wasn't all that interested in chasing that ephemeral emotion.

'Where are we going?' Emma asked, turning from the window to give him a bleakly challenging look.

'A small trattoria I know of,' he replied, and she rolled her eyes, a small huff of laughter escaping her.

'Of course, you know all the best Italian places, don't you?'

That first night they'd met, when he'd taken her to dinner to make it up to her—and because she'd fascinated him—she'd asked him why he'd been in such a hole-in-the-wall place as the bistro where she'd formerly worked. He'd told her it had the most authentic Italian food in New York, and that he made a point of finding all the best restaurants across the world—not the glitziest or most expensive, but the ones that offered the best and most authentic food.

She'd cocked her head, her amber eyes sweeping over him thoughtfully, and he felt as if he'd somehow gone up in her estimation, and the notion had pleased him.

Well, Felix Trattoria in Venice was the best Italian restaurant in Los Angeles, but he didn't care what she thought of it—or him—any more. No matter what the nature of their relationship turned out to be, that kind of emotion was definitely off the table.

They didn't talk for the rest of the short journey to the trattoria in one of LA's most bohemian and laidback neighbourhoods, the restaurant just a few blocks from the beach and boardwalk.

After the driver opened their door, Nico helped Emma out of the car and into the restaurant, to the private table he'd already reserved in the back, a quick call made by his driver on the way over.

'Here we are.'

Emma eyed the table for two set in the secluded alcove askance, and again Nico wondered why she was so reluctant to be in his company. If he'd let himself think about it—and he'd been reeling too much to give it much thought on the twelve-hour plane journey over here—he would have expected her to have some explanation, no matter how absurd, as to why she'd been willing to marry again so quickly. He would have thought she'd try to get him to take her back, crawl on her hands and knees, metaphorically speaking—or maybe not—to get back on the gravy train.

Why wasn't she? What did he not know or understand that would make this situation make sense? Maybe he needed to start with Will, her erstwhile groom.

'Did you love him?' he asked baldly as they sat down, and a discreet waiter laid heavy linen napkins in their laps.

Emma threw him a swift, startled look. 'Love him...'

'Your groom.' He couldn't make himself say his name.

A small sigh escaped her and she looked down at her lap. 'No.'

'So he was just another meal ticket?'

She looked up quickly, her eyes flashing gold at his sneering tone. 'He wasn't, as it happens, but is there something wrong with that?'

'Marrying someone for money? I would say so, yes.'

'Says someone who has never been hungry.' She pressed her lips together and picked up the menu, her stony gaze flicking down its offerings.

Nico found himself in the irritating position of having to backtrack slightly. 'I admit, there is no shame in marrying for money if you are clear that is why you're doing it,' he allowed. 'A marriage of convenience can be a very sensible thing, I'm sure.' Perhaps they would indeed come to a similar arrangement, in time. 'But pretending to care when you don't is reprehensible.' Feeling as if he'd already revealed too much, he picked up his menu.

'And that's what I had with Will,' Emma told him, her tone turning both quiet and fierce. 'We were completely honest with each other from the start. I didn't love him, and he didn't love me, and that was fine. We were just friends, good friends, and it suited us both.'

She put down her menu. 'So perhaps you should stop with your assumptions.'

He hadn't been talking about Will, but that was something he was certainly not going to point out. 'Have you decided what you'd like to eat?' he asked instead.

'I'm not hungry.'

'Emma, don't be childish.'

'I'm not being childish,' she replied, her voice rising. 'I'm actually not hungry.' She glanced away. 'I haven't had much of an appetite lately, as it happens.' She bit her lip, as if she regretted saying that much, and his gaze narrowed.

'More of the flu?' he surmised as he lowered his menu and sat back, his gaze sweeping slowly over her, noting the rush of colour into her cheeks, the way she wouldn't look at him. Every sense prickled with suspicion. What was she hiding? 'Emma?'

A sound escaped her, something between a sigh and a sob. She bowed her head, and the suspicion prickling along the back of his neck sharpened into alarm. Was this the missing piece, the thing he didn't understand? 'Emma,' he said again, this time not a question, but more of a promise, although what he was even promising, he didn't know.

He leaned across the table, brushing her hand with his own. Her skin was so soft and so cold, and he had a sudden urge to wrap his fingers around her own, draw her to him, imbue her with his warmth. The anger he'd been feeling melted in an instant, replaced by a sudden, deep, pervading concern. 'Emma, tell me. Are you ill? Seriously, I mean?' He pictured hospital scenes, shock diagnoses, the secret she'd felt compelled to keep. 'I can arrange the best medical treatment—'

'No, I'm not ill,' she cut across him, 'not unless you count it as an illness.' Her voice was small and sad and defeated, but as she finally looked up at him her eyes still contained that old spark. 'Oh, Nico...the truth is, I'm pregnant.'

CHAPTER FOUR

EMMA LET OUT a laugh at the look of utter and complete shock on Nico's face. It wasn't remotely funny, of course, but laughter had always been her defence, and, in any case, she didn't think she'd ever seen him look so blindsided, so completely pole-axed, as if she'd just hit him over the head with a two-by-four. She shook her head, pressing her hand to her mouth.

'You should see the look on your face,' she told him, and his look of blatant incredulity morphed into a scowl.

'I can well imagine,' he bit out tersely. *'Pregnant.'* He shook his head slowly and Emma dropped her hand from her mouth with a sigh. No, not funny at all, especially when he looked far from pleased, just as she'd feared. Why had she told him? And yet how could she not have?

She knew she'd just taken a huge risk, that this could change everything. Nico, in all his arrogance and pride, would be certain to want to call all the shots about her life, her baby's life. So why *had* she told him? Because, she supposed, she had a core of honour just as he did, even if he would never believe it of her.

And, she acknowledged, because she'd never known her father, and she was reluctant to have her baby not know theirs. And yet…what if that would have been the better choice? The safer one?

Telling him she was pregnant might have been just about the stupidest thing she'd ever done, and yet she couldn't quite make herself regret it.

'So this is why you were marrying that man,' he stated, his gaze sweeping slowly over her.

'Will?' Emma asked, surprised he was making that jump. He hadn't reacted very much to the news he was going to be a father, she acknowledged with a flash of bitterness. 'Yes. I knew I couldn't provide for this baby on my own. I've barely been able to provide for myself.' She lifted her chin, daring him to challenge her. 'Will knew about the baby,' she added. 'He was absolutely fine with it.'

'And yet,' Nico returned scathingly, 'he was willing to walk away quickly enough when he discovered you were married to me. What sort of man does that?'

The condemnation in his voice annoyed her. He was blaming *Will* in this whole fiasco? 'You didn't actually give him much choice,' she pointed out. 'Since you told him to leave. And why wouldn't he? What else was he supposed to do, when we obviously couldn't marry, after all, since I was already married to you?' She would have to text Will and explain, she realised, dreading that conversation, even over the phone. Poor Will. He'd been so kind to her, and this was a horrible way to repay him. She would have to find some way to explain.

'I would think,' Nico returned coolly, 'or at least

hope, that a man would have more regard for his own child.'

She stared at him—those cool green eyes, now narrowed; the full, sculpted lips pressed together in censure—and realised the assumption he'd made. He thought *Will* was the father, and although his presumption absolutely infuriated her, she recognised, reluctantly, that it was not an entirely unfounded conclusion to draw. She knew she wasn't showing very much yet; the obstetrician had said she was small for fourteen weeks, mainly because of the debilitating morning sickness she'd had since the beginning.

Staring at Nico, knowing what he now believed, she was tempted, treacherously, to let him go on believing it. Why shouldn't she, after all? He was controlling, suspicious, and right now he seemed as if he hated her—hardly the kind of father she wanted for her baby, or, for that matter, husband for herself. Why not walk away if she could?

Nico, Emma knew, had just given her the only out she could possibly take. If he believed she was pregnant with another man's child, he would almost definitely divorce her, as he'd already said he intended to do. Wasn't that really the best thing for both of them? He was never going to love or trust her again, not that she even wanted him to, of course, and she didn't love or trust him, anyway. Not any more. That kind of suspicion was hardly the best basis for a marriage, a family, and, anyway, she knew she'd always done better on her own. She'd stayed strong, safe, smart. She should walk away now, for the sake of her baby. *Their* baby...

which was why she closed her eyes, let out a long, defeated sigh.

'Nico…the baby isn't Will's.' She parted with each word reluctantly, wondering even as she spoke if she was making a huge mistake. Another one. She was used to being tough, taking it on the chin, and looking out for herself, so why she was breaking all her rules now, she had no idea. Maybe because she'd never known her own father. She couldn't do the same to her own child…or to Nico. Even if it would be smarter to.

'Another man, then?' His nostrils flared and his mouth tightened. 'You do work fast, Emma. Faster even than I realised, it seems.' His voice vibrated with anger, and suddenly Emma found herself matching his fury. *That* was where he went with this? Yet another man? They'd been at it non-stop for their whole affair, why would it not occur to him that he, her *husband*, was the father?

'You really are remarkably insulting,' she snapped. 'I have to say, it's a real talent, along with making assumptions, which is what you've done since you marched into my wedding—'

He leaned across the table, his eyes flashing jade. 'A wedding that never should have happened!'

'You were *dead*!' The words seemed to echo through the restaurant, followed by the loud and obvious sound of someone clearing his throat. Emma glanced over and saw a white-jacketed server waiting to take their order, struggling to keep a bland look on his face. An unruly laugh escaped her and she put her hand over her mouth while Nico glared first at her, and then the waiter.

'We'll both have the *strangulet*,' he bit out. 'And mineral water, please.'

'I told you, I'm not hungry,' Emma protested, although now that her stomach was empty, she actually did think she could manage some food. She knew she should eat for the sake of her baby, yet she couldn't bring herself to bow to Nico's wishes yet again, even about something so small.

'You need to eat,' he returned with a quelling look. 'And the *strangulet* is the best thing on the menu. Besides, it's not too rich or spicy, so it should be appropriate.'

The waiter silently took their menus as Emma leaned back in her chair. Even when he was being thoughtful, Nico made assumptions. Acted arrogantly. The man really was impossible. She would be well rid of him.

He'd been like that before, she remembered, calling all the shots, although considering the luxury he'd showered her with, she hadn't minded too much. That first night he'd wined and dined her, and then, as it had been so late, he'd insisted she stay the night. A gentleman, he hadn't touched her then, but, looking back, Emma saw he'd still acted with the arrogance that that moment would surely come—when he said it would.

When they had begun their affair, he'd made it clear it was a temporary arrangement; she was only there at his behest, for as long as he decided it would last. He'd arranged everything—their accommodation, travel, even what she wore, ate, drank, did. She'd been, Emma acknowledged bitterly, like a doll he could dress up and play with, and she hadn't minded because the world he'd introduced her to had been so glamorous and intoxicating, unlike anything she'd ever known. She'd just been along for the wondrous ride, caught up in the fairy tale even as she tried to caution herself that, like everything else in her life, it wouldn't last.

Their whole relationship—the single month of it—had been out of time, away from reality. First in New York, staying in the most opulent hotel Emma could have ever imagined, and then in Rome, at his palatial penthouse flat. She hadn't even had a passport before she'd met him. She hadn't been anywhere, done anything, besides simply try to survive, and yet he'd opened worlds to her, with the travel, the luxury, the amazing food, the attention.

So many worlds…including the intoxicating one of passion. But she really could not let herself be distracted by the memories of *that* right now.

'So this Will was amenable to marrying you even though you were pregnant with another man's child,' Nico surmised, shaking his head, clearly finding the notion incredible, and, no doubt, repellent.

'Yes, he was.' She was too angry to bother correcting Nico right now, and in her fury she wasn't even sure that she should. The assumptions he made were really beyond the pale.

The waiter came back to fill their water glasses, and Emma took a much-needed sip. Her throat felt terribly dry, and her heart was hammering. She took a steadying breath. 'He didn't want to marry anyone at all, wasn't interested in a romantic relationship, but his mother kept pressuring him, pretty unbearably. He's a shy, mild sort of guy, and he couldn't take it. So this was the solution.' And it had worked—or at least it *would* have worked—admirably for both of them. 'It was an amicable arrangement, based on companionship, nothing more,' she told Nico. 'Like I said, it suited us both.' And she would need to talk to Will and explain everything as soon as she could. He deserved that much, at the very least.

Nico didn't look particularly impressed by her words. Emma had a feeling that right now Nico wouldn't believe her if she told him the sky was blue. It was a wearying thought.

'And what of the child?' he asked. 'He was willing to raise it as his own, act as its father?'

Emma swallowed, nodded. All right, she'd been too angry to correct Nico, it was true, but this was starting to feel uncomfortably like lying. She really needed to tell him the truth, or at least decide for herself whether she was going to tell him. The longer she strung this out, the more furious he would be at her seeming deception...if he ever found out. And he would find out, because she really didn't think she could keep such a huge secret from him. Besides, she was terrible at lying. But as she considered all she stood to lose the words wouldn't come. 'Yes, he was,' she managed finally. 'Like I said, he's a good man.'

She'd met Will at a party she'd been hired to waitress for; he'd been at the bar, drinking steadily, and had, in something of a stupor, told her all about his controlling mother and the desire to simply live his life without her relentless interference. He was utterly committed to his work as a software engineer, and wasn't interested in any romantic relationships, although he thought he wouldn't mind having children one day.

Emma, having just discovered, to her great shock, that she was pregnant, had been wondering how on earth she was going to manage. She'd been living in a bedsit, enduring the usual hand-to-mouth existence, trying to eke out the money Nico's cousin had given her before she'd left. And yet despite all that she'd known, absolutely, that she wanted this baby. She wanted someone to love, someone to be hers. A family, at last, like she'd never, ever known. The family she'd always longed for.

She'd joked to Will that they should marry—and yes, it *had* been a joke, if a somewhat desperate one. To her utter surprise, Will had taken her at her word. He'd given her his card and asked for her number, and Emma had assumed that would be that—a drunken conversation, nothing more—when he'd texted her the next day.

Are you serious?

And she realised she had been. She'd had to be, because she didn't have any other options, and now she had someone else to think about. Someone so very important.

They'd spent a couple of weeks getting to know each other, and Will had been a reassuringly open book, a workaholic with a few, simple pleasures, happy to chat but generally enjoying his own company. He'd asked for a prenup, which had made sense, and told her she could redecorate his apartment in Santa Monica if

she liked, as long as she left his study alone. He'd liked
the idea of a baby, and had even come along to her
first scan two weeks ago. They had never been going
to have a great passion, or any passion, but that had
been fine. After Nico, Emma wasn't ready to deal with
that kind of explosive chemistry again, or any kind of
chemistry, and Will really was happy in his own company. Emma had her baby to think about, and that had
felt like enough. More than enough. Their marriage
would have been simple and unexciting and *safe*.

And now it was over. The future she'd so carefully
tried to construct blasted into smithereens…by the
man sitting across from her.

'You look so sad,' Nico remarked mockingly. 'Are
you missing him?'

'He's a kind man, and as you said, he was willing
to take on another man's child,' Emma returned tartly,
'so yes, I am. He was a good friend.'

'And the father?' Nico asked. 'Another man who
was your mark, I suppose?'

Her *mark*? What did he think she was, Mata Hari?
She let out a disbelieving huff of laughter as she shook
her head. 'I'd find your cynicism amusing,' she told
him before she could think better of it, 'if it wasn't
so pathetic.'

Anger flashed in his eyes and the skin around his
mouth went rather alarmingly white. 'Don't test me,
Emma.'

She shouldn't be so flippant or foolhardy, Emma
knew. As tender as Nico had seemed during their
whirlwind courtship and marriage, he was also a man
who was known to be ruthless in business, who knew

what he wanted and how to get it—and discard it, if he so chose. She'd looked him up, after the crash, and seen the trail of affairs and broken hearts he'd left behind him, a string of casual affairs that had made headlines. She hadn't been surprised, but it hardly inspired confidence now.

'How far along are you?' he asked, sitting back in his seat, his arms folded. 'Out of interest?'

She hesitated, her mind racing between viable options. Lie, and protect herself and her baby. Tell the truth…and take the consequences, whatever they might be. It felt, she thought despairingly, no choice at all.

'Well?' Nico prompted.

'Not…' She swallowed hard. 'Not very far along.'

Not very far along? Why didn't she know? Had there been that many men? No matter what he'd learned of her, Nico couldn't quite make himself believe that. When he'd taken her in his arms for the first time, she'd seemed remarkably innocent, and so very sweet. So very different from the women he usually took to his bed, who were as pragmatic as he was when it came to matters of the heart. He remembered the moment with Emma perfectly—it had been three days after they'd met. She had confessed she'd had nowhere to go and so Nico had told her she could stay in his hotel suite. He hadn't been leaving New York for a week, after all, and he'd felt badly for, admittedly indirectly, causing her to lose her job. He'd been determined to be the perfect gentleman and he had been, even as his attraction for Emma had threatened to overwhelm him.

Her whimsical guilelessness or *seeming* guileless-ness—he knew better now—had won him over. After the lies of his childhood, his mother's damning silence, his father's painful coldness, here was someone simple and innocent and pure. Ha! As if. Had Emma actually been orchestrating their first encounter, when she'd stood on her tiptoes and brushed a kiss across his mouth? Had she just been pretending when he'd looked down at her, his heart starting to hammer in expectation, and she'd smiled so softly, so tremulously?

And when he'd asked, his voice already raw with wanting, throbbing with need, 'Are you sure?' she'd exhaled on a small sigh of surrender.

'Yes...'

Had that all been faked? And yet what had happened after hadn't been. He knew that absolutely. He remembered the feel of her beneath him, open and pliant, writhing and wanting. The explosion when they came together had rocked them both to the core, left them gasping and clutching each other as if they were the last bits of wreckage on a drowning sea. And when he'd looked down at her, smiling in a sort of wry disbelief, she'd laughed, a sound of pure joy.

'*Wow...*' she'd breathed, and he'd grinned, rolling onto his back, taking her with him, his arms clasped around her, sexual satiation combined with a soul-deep contentment.

No, Nico decided, some things could *not* be faked.

And yet right now Emma was definitely looking shifty. She kept her gaze lowered as she took little sips of water, her fingers trembling around her glass.

What more could she possibly be hiding? Who *was* the father?

In one sudden, swift movement, Nico leaned forward, and captured her wrist in his hand, removing the glass with the other. 'What is it that you're keeping from me, Emma?' he asked in a low voice. 'Because it's obviously something. I've never seen you look so... so *scared* before.' He'd never seen her look scared at all. He'd always admired her spirit, her strength. Where had it gone? What had spooked her? Or was this too some sort of act?

He'd thought, for a few wondrous seconds, when she'd first told him she was pregnant, that she'd meant *he* was the father, and his heart had leapt with a wild mix of elation and amazement. A child of his own. It had been an unlikely notion, he knew, because she didn't look pregnant, and she'd have to be at least three months along—three and a *half* months—for him to be the father. Besides, they'd used protection assiduously. He'd made sure of that.

Then he'd realised, in the space of a single heartbeat, by the resigned look on her face, that of course he wasn't. She hadn't wanted to tell him about her pregnancy, he'd realised, because carrying another man's child would make her less attractive to him, understandably so. The disappointment that had thudded through him he'd pushed away resolutely. No need to feel that, all things considered.

And, he realised, it now all made an awful sort of sense—pregnant with another man's child, she'd known all along that he wouldn't want her back. No wonder she'd seemed reluctant, and yes, even scared that he'd returned. *That* was the secret she'd been keeping…but now that he knew, why did she still look fearful? Could there be more?

Emma glanced down at his fingers encircling her wrist, her face pale and drawn. He could feel her pulse fluttering beneath his thumb, and, without even thinking about what he was doing, he stroked the silky skin there, letting his thumb linger on her cool, soft flesh. A shudder escaped her, her expression turning dazed, and desire ignited low in his belly. One tiny, treacherous touch, and already he felt lost with wanting her. Remembering how it had been between them, overwhelming his senses, making him forget everything else. His mother's betrayal. His father's indifference. The sense of spinning in emptiness that he'd felt, not knowing who he was, where he came from or where he belonged. The world he'd wanted to walk away from as he'd forged a new one with her.

Lies, so many painful lies, but right now all he could remember was how her arms had felt around him, her body pliant and sweetly yielding beneath his as she'd gasped out his name…

'Please let me go,' she whispered.

After another heated beat he released her wrist and sat back. Emma cradled her arm against her chest, as if he'd hurt her. He knew he hadn't; he could see from her dilated pupils and flushed face that such a simple touch had affected her, too, the way it had him. She remembered how it had been between them, as well. The chemistry between them was just as strong even now, after she'd told him she was pregnant with another man's child. The realisation was both shaming and infuriating.

And yet…there were worse things, far worse, to build a marriage on than chemistry.

He let the possibility linger in his mind, just as it had before. Yes, admittedly the child was a complication he hadn't foreseen, and he, of all people, knew how difficult it was to take on another man's child, yet also, perhaps, potentially rewarding? Here, possibly, was a way to redeem the past… He could love this child the way he never had been. He could give it a hope and a future. Was he strong enough to do that? Did he want to?

His mind raced with new possibilities—Emma as his wife, in all senses of the word, or almost. Love, obviously, would not be part of this complicated equation. And her child—*his* child, or would be. He'd adopt it, naturally, as soon as possible. Treat it like his own in every way…if he could.

'Why are you looking at me like that?' Emma asked shakily, and Nico refocussed his gaze on her. The colour had receded from her cheeks, leaving her pale and drawn again, and she was still cradling her arm against her chest.

'I am considering our future,' he told her matter-of-factly.

'Our future? And what are you considering, exactly?' she asked, clearly trying to sound braver than she felt. She released her arm, resting her slender hand on the table, fingers spread as if to anchor herself.

'I didn't expect the child,' he admitted frankly. 'It has, to put it mildly, put a spanner in the works.'

She let out a choked sound, something not quite a laugh, but at least not a sob. 'A spanner in what works, Nico?'

'Our marriage.' He frowned, considering the ramifications. Could he really take on another man's child? He knew the pain and heartache that could cause, on both sides, and in truth he wasn't completely sure if he could love another man's child the way he would love his own. Shaming to admit, especially considering his own birth, but he knew he needed to be honest with himself. The last thing he wanted to do was act as his father had—be cold to the child entrusted to him, give it less than he or she deserved simply because of an accident of biology, of blood. The way he had been, although he knew he couldn't actually fault his father for excluding him. He'd included him in the family business—grudgingly, reluctantly, but he had. But Nico had always still felt the loss, the confusion at not understanding why his father could barely endure his presence...until his mother had, on her deathbed, hurled a grenade into their family, causing an explosion that still ricocheted through him to this day.

'What about our marriage?' Emma asked.

'Whether it continues.' His frown deepened as he realised fully that he couldn't walk away from his wife, even when she was pregnant with another man's child. He didn't even want to. 'The father,' he asked. 'Does he know about the child? Did you tell him? Why did he not take responsibility?' The man was clearly either in the dark or a complete cad.

'I...' Emma didn't have a chance to reply, for the waiter came with their meals then—two steaming plates of *strangulet*, tube-like pasta with fresh tomato, basil and garlic. They were both silent as he set the plates down before them and then, with a murmur of thanks, left them alone.

Emma's head was bent as she picked up her fork and toyed with the pasta on her plate, her brow furrowed.

'Well?' Nico prompted. 'Did you tell him?'

'I never had the opportunity,' she half mumbled, her head still bent over the plate.

'Never? Why not?'

'He...disappeared before I could.'

She sounded mortified, as if each word were painful to say, and so it would be, when he considered what she was confessing. A one-night stand, just about as soon as he'd been declared dead? He'd been missing for how long by then? A few weeks? A month? He swallowed down his anger.

'I see.'

Emma let out a wavery laugh. 'You really don't.'

'So tell me, then.' Nico heard the anger thrumming in his voice, and he knew Emma did, as well. 'And *look* at me, for heaven's sake, Emma. Or are you so embarrassed about your own behaviour you can't bear to look me in the eye?'

'I'm not embarrassed,' Emma retorted, looking up so he could see the golden flash of her eyes, 'although perhaps *you* should be, at your absurdly high-handed manner, making all these judgments and assumptions about me. If I'd known just how absurdly arrogant you were, I wouldn't have married you in the first place!'

He reared back, her response only adding to his

anger. 'Oh, really? I'm just trying to find answers. Answers you seem suspiciously reluctant to give—'

'Oh, Nico.' Emma let out a laugh that definitely sounded more like a sob as she dropped her head into her hands. 'For heaven's *sake*. I cannot continue this ridiculous pretence any longer. I don't know why I even tried, except...' She trailed off, swallowing, and he tensed, annoyance flaring within him along with the anger, although he wasn't even sure what exactly to be annoyed about. 'Why don't you just tell me straight, for once, then?' he demanded.

She looked up again, bleakly this time, her eyes full of weary resignation. 'Nico, there isn't another man. Not Will, not some stranger or whoever you are imagining in your unending cynicism. *You're* the father of this baby.'

CHAPTER FIVE

AND SO THE die was cast. Amidst the fear and uncertainty, Emma felt a flicker of relief. She really had never been good at lying, which had certainly got her into trouble as a kid. She couldn't pretend she hadn't stolen food, or cheated on her homework, or done whatever she'd had to, to keep body and soul together. The result had been she'd been labelled a troublemaker from the get-go, which was not great when you were being cycled through the foster system, one family after another, each one passing you on like a parcel they didn't want. And probably not so great here, considering she'd just handed Nico all the cards, do with them what he would.

But what else could she have done? She'd tried—sort of—to go along with his assumption that there was another man, but it had been too hard—and too insulting. She'd seen the way his nostrils had flared and his lips had tightened at the thought of her sleeping around, never mind his own colourful past. He could have a dozen or more casual affairs, it seemed, but heaven forbid if she did. In any case, it seemed her husband had no trouble believing all manner of things about her—well, what else was new? Nico Santini was just showing he was like everybody else. She'd lived the fairy tale for a month, but it was now well and truly over.

Except she was still married to Nico...and he now knew he was the father of her baby. Another fairy tale might be starting, of the Brothers Grimm variety, scary ending included. Emma's stomach tightened with anxiety.

'Mine?' Nico repeated, his voice filled with icy disbelief. 'Impossible.'

So now that she'd told him, he was going to deny it? 'Impossible?' she repeated, letting a huff of hard laughter. 'Not if you know about the birds and the bees, which I'm pretty sure you do.'

Annoyance flashed across his features. 'Don't be facetious, Emma—'

'Trust me, I'm not.' She shook her head slowly, wondering why he found it so hard to believe, when they'd been together for a whole month. Yes, he'd used protection, but everyone knew protection could fail, and there had been more than a few times when they'd both been in an eager rush, fumbling in their passionate haste, as she remembered all too well. Even now just a memory of such an encounter had heat blooming low in her belly, between her thighs. Unhelpful at this particular moment. *Very* unhelpful.

And yet all he really had to do, she reflected bitterly, was the maths. Did he really distrust her that much?

'Nico,' she said wearily, 'you are definitely the father, I promise. There hasn't been another man since you, so, really, you are absolutely the only candidate.'

Make of that what he would, although from the blatant scepticism on his face, he was struggling to believe that, as well, and Emma wished she hadn't told him quite so much. She was feeling vulnerable enough already, even if he couldn't see it.

'I'm the father,' he stated incredulously, as if daring her to throw her hands up and admit she was lying.

Jokes! You're actually not. Fooled you for a second, though, didn't I?

'Yes, the father,' she repeated, rolling her eyes, an edge to her voice, because he was really milking this whole incredulity thing just a little too much. 'I don't know why you're *quite* so sceptical. The dates do match up—'

He shook his head, determined to believe the absolute worst of her, it seemed. Well, most people did, but for some reason, stupidly, with Nico it hurt more. 'You said you weren't far along—'

'I'm fourteen weeks.'

His dark brow came together in a scowl as realisation dawned, a blazing light in his eyes, a tautening of his mouth. 'So what you actually mean is, you lied earlier.'

'I didn't lie,' she protested, knowing she was now on shaky ground. 'I was just…sparing with the truth.' Very sparing, but only for about half an hour. She couldn't have managed much more, she knew, as much as she might have wanted to.

'But why?' He slapped his palm against the table, startling her with the loud crack of sound, as colour slashed those magnificent cheekbones. He was, she realised, trembling inwardly, truly angry. Angrier, even, than when he'd stormed into her wedding, as she'd tried to marry another man. Was this about pride— or something else? It reminded her, painfully, that she really didn't know him at all, and once again she wondered if she'd just made a big, big mistake, trusting him with the truth of their child.

'Why would you lie about that?' he demanded. 'What purpose would it possibly serve?'

'You jumped to conclusions,' Emma replied, trying to rally. She was not entirely at fault here, for the misunderstanding. 'First thinking it was Will's, and then some…some stranger's! Thanks, by the way, for assuming I really get around. And that's not even considering the sexism of it being okay for *you* to get around but not me.'

'We're not talking about me right now, and what was I supposed to think, when you did not correct me?' he returned, his voice rising. 'And you married within three months of—'

'Three and a half months,' Emma interjected with biting, saccharine sweetness. He was angry? Well, so was she.

'Enough!' he commanded in a freezing tone. 'If the child is mine, I assumed you would have told me right at the start, not prevaricated in order to keep the truth from me. The fact that you didn't made me assume it was not, which, I believe, is entirely and unfortunately understandable.' His eyes narrowed, his mouth thinning. 'Indeed, I am still sceptical, all things considered. Why *wouldn't* you tell me, Emma, for heaven's sake?'

'Oh, good *grief*.' She shook her head as she threw

her napkin on top of the table, too weary to keep going around in circles, trying to convince him. 'I've had enough of this.'

'Emma—'

'I'm leaving,' she stated, stalking from the table on unsteady legs. Tears blurred her eyes and she blinked them back. It was ridiculous to feel so hurt. Nico didn't trust her? Well, she didn't trust him. A perfect match, then. As if.

'Emma, stop.'

She heard Nico push back his chair as she kept walking, towards the front of the restaurant. Not, she realised belatedly, that she had anywhere to go. She was supposed to be staying with Will tonight; he'd moved all her stuff—which admittedly was only a couple of suitcases—to his apartment yesterday. She supposed she could go there and throw herself on his mercy, but it felt presumptuous, considering all that had happened. But where else could she go?

'Emma, wait.'

She was at the front door when Nico grabbed her arm, turned her around to face him. 'Don't storm out of here in a huff—'

'I'm not in a *huff*,' she snapped. 'I'm just really tired of you doubting me constantly. And I'm tired full stop, because, you know, I'm *pregnant*, and I want to go somewhere and sleep, so can you please just leave me alone?' She tried to shake off his arm, but he wouldn't let her.

'I'm not leaving you alone,' Nico gritted as he steered her out of the front door, away from the prying eyes of the other diners. They were creating quite a scene. 'You're my *wife*.'

They stood on the sidewalk outside the trattoria, a balmy breeze from the ocean buffeting them, Nico still holding her arm. Emma closed her eyes as a wave of fatigue crashed over her. She was so not up for this. She'd been through the emotional wringer today, and, as much as she prided herself on quick thinking and good survival skills, right now she felt completely tapped out. She couldn't summon her usual insouciance, that determined, daredevil laugh, the eyebrow arched in challenge. She just couldn't.

'What do you want from me, Nico?' she asked wearily, her eyes still closed. 'Just tell me that, at least. What do you want from me right now?'

'I...' He sounded surprised by the question, baffled even, and she opened her eyes to find him staring at her, so clearly at a loss. 'Look,' he said finally, 'you're obviously exhausted, and you need somewhere to stay. Let's go back to my hotel. We can have these conversations later.'

As if on cue, his car glided up to the kerb and the driver hopped out. Emma hesitated, because she didn't really want to roll over and let Nico call all the shots *again*, but she knew she needed a break from the intensity, as well as some sleep, and it was getting late. Maybe tomorrow she'd stumble on a solution she couldn't seem to find now. She'd figure out a way to have this all make sense.

'All right,' she agreed, not all that graciously.

The driver opened the back door of the car and Nico helped her inside. Emma leaned her back against the sumptuous leather as Nico settled himself next to her and the driver closed the door.

'Where are you staying?' she asked, and he named one of the city's most modern and luxurious hotels, in Beverly Hills, of course. Emma had walked by it a couple of times, awed by its tinted windows and sweeping arcs of glass and chrome, a testament to innovation. Nico had always had a taste for culture, a preference for the best. Some things, it seemed, hadn't changed.

It was the last thought that flickered through Emma's mind before, thanks to the soft leather seat and the smooth rolling of the car, she fell gratefully into a doze, the cares slipping from her for a few blessed moments.

Nico stared at Emma, now curled on her side, her head drooping towards her knees, already deeply asleep after just a few minutes in the car. He felt a sudden and surprisingly strong flare of protectiveness for her, looking so tired and so vulnerable. Was she really telling the truth about this child? She seemed to be, but still he was wary. He knew he had good reason to be, considering the situation. And, he acknowledged, reasons that had nothing to do with Emma and that she wouldn't understand. Reasons that still hurt to think about too deeply, when he considered the yawning abyss of knowledge of his own parentage. Now, with his mother dead, he would never know.

But his own child would.

He'd make sure of that.

He should, he supposed, make this simple, and order a paternity test. There was no reason not to, although he wondered if Emma would balk at such a request. But if she was being honest, then surely she wouldn't? And if the child really *was* his...

He realised that flare of protectiveness he felt was not just for Emma, his wife, but for his child.

His child.

A sense of incredulity, of wonder and hope, flooded through him, buoyed his soul. His own flesh and blood, unlike any other. Someone to love, to protect, to cherish. For ever.

If Emma was telling the truth...

Was he wrong, to doubt her so much? He thought of his cousin dismissing her as a gold-digger, with the cold, hard proof, after all, that she'd insisted on leaving, had taken the money Antonio had offered. And, all right, maybe she *had* married him for money, back then; she certainly didn't seem to be denying it now. But that, in itself, was a certain kind of honesty, and besides, she surely had to know that he could order a paternity test and sort this out in a matter of days. Why would she keep lying?

'Signor?'

Nico was startled from his thoughts by the driver, who had pulled up to the front of the hotel without him even realising.

'Thank you, Paulo.'

'The *signora*?' he asked, nodding towards Emma, still curled up on the back seat.

'I'll take care of her,' Nico replied, realising he meant it in every sense of the word. He got out of the car without Emma so much as stirring, and then, as gently as he could, scooped her up into his arms. She was light—so light!—and she curled into him unthinkingly, her head nestled against his chest. He breathed her in, smiling when he realised she still smelled of soap. Eau de Dollar Store, indeed. It was a heady fragrance.

'I can walk…' she mumbled sleepily, without moving, and Nico's arms tightened around her.

'It's fine,' he said gruffly. In truth, it was more than fine. She was a delectable armful, curled into him, her breasts pressed against his chest, his hands skimming her curves as he hoisted her securely against him. Desire stirred, a persistent ache in his groin, forcing him to shift his tempting bundle. He was not about to complicate things with that element, as wonderful as it had been. Not yet, anyway.

He strode through the ultra-modern foyer, all marble and glass, causing a few raised eyebrows and curious stares, and into the private lift that soared up eighteen flights, directly to the penthouse suite, which took up the entire top floor.

Stepping inside, he deposited Emma gently on one of the cream leather sofas scattered across the black marble floor of the soaring living space, floor-to-ceiling windows giving views of the city in every direction, so it almost felt like being suspended in mid-air.

As he stepped back she lifted her head, blinking the room into focus.

'Wow.' Slowly she looked around, taking in the mahogany bar, the grand piano, the priceless modern sculpture scattered about, and, most of all, the three-hundred-and-sixty-degree view. 'Some place.'

'Do you want to go to bed?' He'd meant the question innocently, but heat flooded his face—and his groin—at the mere mention of those evocative words. Seeing Emma sitting there, tousle-haired and sleepy-eyed, was firing his blood. Everywhere. 'I mean,' he corrected tautly, 'do you want to go to sleep.'

A small, playful smile curved Emma's mouth as she glanced at him from underneath her lashes, golden eyes glinting, before the smile dropped and she sighed. 'I know what you meant. And actually, in all honesty, what I'd really like is a bath. I'm assuming this place has some ridiculously huge, sunken tub? Marble, with jets?' She raised her eyebrows impishly and he found himself smiling back, even laughing a little.

'Of course it does.'

'Excellent.' She stretched, her yellow dress pulling taut across her breasts, making him ache all the more, before she stood up. 'Bring it on, then.'

Nico did his best to keep things matter-of-fact as he showed her the master bath, attached to the bedroom with its tempting, king-sized bed. The only bed in the suite as it happened, but they'd cross that rather interesting bridge when they came to it.

The bathroom was fitted out just as Emma had hoped—with a huge sunken tub of black marble and many jets. 'There's a dressing gown on the door,' he told her. 'And plenty of toiletries there, on the shelf. If there's anything else you need...'

'My stuff, I suppose,' she replied. 'I don't actually have any clothes with me besides this dress.'

'Where are your things?'

'At Will's apartment, in Santa Monica.'

He kept his expression neutral although he realised he hated the thought of her belongings there, *her* there. She would have been right now, as the man's wife, if he hadn't come into the church and disrupted the wedding. The thought was enough to make him grit his teeth, but he forced himself to relax. It hadn't happened. She was here, with him, and it was their future he had to focus on. Their child.

'If you give me the address,' he told her, 'I'll have Paulo fetch them for you and bring them here.'

She hesitated, and then nodded once, seemingly reluctantly. 'All right. Thank you.'

'Do you want to get them yourself?' he surmised, a bit sharply, and she sighed.

'No, Nico, not particularly, but I do feel I owe Will an explanation. He is a good, kind man, and I basically dumped him in it, deserting him at the altar.'

'With good cause.'

'Still, he deserves a conversation. I should call him tonight.' She glanced around, her eyes widening in sudden realisation. 'I just remembered, I left my bag at the church, with my phone and wallet—'

'Paulo retrieved your belongings from the church earlier. They're in the car. I'll have them brought up to you.'

She hesitated, seeming as if she wanted to argue the point, and then she nodded. 'Thank you.'

He paused and then said quietly, 'I know I've been angry, Emma, but I'm not some kind of monster here. I am trying to be reasonable about all this.' As hard as that was. He supposed he could ease up, a little.

'I know,' she said quietly, but she didn't sound particularly convinced, and he had the sense that it was as hard for her to trust him as it was for him to trust her. Yet had he really ever given her any reason to doubt him?

'Enjoy your bath,' he said, and then left, closing the door behind him. He heard her turn the lock with an audible click.

Out in the living area, Nico poured himself a healthy measure of whisky from the decanter on the bar and then stepped outside to the wraparound balcony, the glittering lights of Los Angeles spread all around him, the ocean a blanket of darkness in the distance. He breathed in deeply and let it out in a rush as the events of the last few days caught up with him, leaving him wrung out and just about as exhausted as Emma.

Less than a week ago he'd been in Jakarta, his memory coming back to him over the course of a difficult month, first in vague fragments and confusing pieces, and then with more clarity and precision. He'd remembered Emma first; when the rest of his life had remained cloudy and unfocussed, she had stood out like a beacon of hope, a shining angel.

He was embarrassed now to recall just how much he had clung to her memory, how he'd felt it had helped him to recover. When he'd been struggling to walk, to focus, to so much as think clearly, he'd pictured their future together, their joyous reunion, her incredulous wonder at finding out he was alive, and it had compelled him onward.

The fact that reality had been so far removed from his absurd fairy-tale fantasy had made him, he realised, a bit angrier and more accusing with her than he might have been otherwise. Than perhaps he should have been. Still, the discovery of her wedding, her betrayal, her shameless admission of marrying him for money…it all stung, still.

Two weeks ago he'd finally been in touch with his cousin, Antonio, who had been shocked to hear of his survival, and then, belatedly, pleased. Nico knew there was no love lost between them; Antonio would always be angry that his father had chosen him, the cuckoo in the nest, over his own blood, even if he'd only done it to save himself the humiliation of admitting to the world his wife had betrayed him.

When he'd returned to Italy, he'd received the news, from a rather smugly certain Antonio, of what really had happened after his alleged death. How Emma had demanded money from him immediately after the memorial service. How she hadn't wanted to be in touch, hadn't wanted anything to do with his family at all, just the cold, hard cash. Antonio had given her ten thousand dollars, a paltry amount really, but Nico supposed he understood his cousin's reluctance to offer more to someone who had clearly revealed herself as nothing more than a shameless gold-digger…just as he'd said she was.

And yet Emma had taken it, so Antonio had indicated, and gladly, considering the prenup he'd had her sign before their whirlwind wedding—the one spot of sense in his dazed unreality. She would have been entitled to more than ten grand, though, he realised, so sloping off with that relatively paltry amount of money, he mused now, was hardly the action of a gold-digger, at least not a very ambitious one—something he hadn't considered in his anger and hurt, when he'd learned from Antonio that she was marrying again. So what was really going on? Or maybe ten grand had seemed like a pretty good deal to her. He really didn't know.

What this all showed him, he thought as he tossed back the last of his whisky, was that he really didn't know his wife at all. And whether he could trust her remained to be seen. But if she was having his child, he would have to remedy both those situations as soon as he possibly could.

CHAPTER SIX

EMMA LEANED HER head back against the cool marble of the sunken tub and closed her eyes, enjoying the sensation of the hot, bubbly, rose-scented water frothing about her, her muscles starting to relax, her bones to melt. This was, she acknowledged ruefully, about as close to heaven as she could get right now. If only she could stay in this lovely warm bath for ever and forget the world—and the man—awaiting her on the other side of the bathroom door.

Unfortunately she couldn't. Her temples throbbed even as her body relaxed, and she wondered—again—whether she'd made a mistake in telling Nico about the baby. Well, she told herself, doing her best to be pragmatic as she opened her eyes and gazed about the opulent bathroom with its black marble and gold fixtures, the reality was, mistake it might be, but she'd made it. She'd told Nico he was the father of her child, whether he believed her or not, and she now had to deal with the fallout. Would Nico come round or would he stay suspicious? Would he keep her in his life so they could attempt to be some sort of family? Was that something she even wanted to risk?

A shudder of apprehension went through her, and she tipped her head back against the tub and closed her eyes once more. She couldn't think about all that just yet. One day at a time, one minute at a time, was the most she could manage if she wanted to hold onto her sanity. Eventually she would formulate a plan, a way forward she could live with. Hopefully. Right now, though, she was too tired, and all out of ideas.

Her hand crept to the slight, reassuring swell of her middle. 'I'm trying to keep you safe, little one,' she murmured. 'I really am.' Unfortunately, she still had to figure out just how to do that, with Nico now in the picture.

What, she wondered with a bittersweet pang, would have happened if he hadn't been in that plane crash? Would they have continued in their idyllic, time-out-of-reality way for much longer? Surely that fairy tale couldn't have lasted for ever. For the month she'd been with him she'd been sure it would end at any moment, that Nico would glance at her with a resigned sort of smile and say, *It was fun, but...*

Instead he'd asked her to marry him. She remembered the moment perfectly, as if it were engraved in her mind with crystalline clarity—she'd been on the balcony of his palatial apartment in Rome, gazing out at the ancient city streets, the Forum in the distance twinkling with its own lights. She'd had to pinch herself, quite literally, because she couldn't believe she was standing there, in such luxurious circumstances, with a man who made her head spin and her heart beat hard. Not, of course, that she'd had any intention of falling in love with him. She knew better than that.

And yet…she'd been close, alarmingly close, simply because he'd been so kind to her.

Since she'd met him—well, truthfully, fifteen minutes after—Nico Santini had showered her with attention, care, interest and compassion. For someone who had learned to live life on her own a long time ago, it had been a much-needed, and rather frightening, balm to her soul. So she'd stood on the balcony and cautioned herself to be careful, to stay cautious.

Then Nico had walked onto the balcony, taken her into his arms, and murmured against her hair, 'Emma, marry me.'

Emma had stiffened in his embrace, utterly shocked. She'd never, not for one moment, not for one *second*, thought their fling was actually going anywhere. Nico Santini, hot billionaire, was amusing himself with the likes of her for a little while, and that was fine. *Fine.* She was of the take-what-you-can-get school of thinking. She'd had to be.

As Nico's arms had tightened around her, she'd eased back to gaze up into his face, searching his intent expression for clues.

'You aren't serious.'

'I am.'

He'd sounded so heartfelt. She'd been completely confused. 'Why?' she'd asked, meaning the question genuinely. Utterly.

'We've had fun these last few weeks, haven't we?'

'Yes, but…' That was all it had been. *Fun.* You didn't get married because you'd had *fun*. A man like Nico—wealthy, powerful, sexy as all get-out—didn't actually *marry* someone like her. He just didn't. Emma had known that. She'd understood it, accepted it, and she'd thought Nico had, as well. And yet there he was, holding her in his arms, asking her *that* question.

'Marry me, Emma,' he'd said again, sounding so much as if he'd really meant it, and even though she couldn't understand why he'd want to, the second time he'd asked she hadn't been able to resist. Even if it had made sense to be cautious. Even if it had been smart to guard her heart. How could a girl like her, who'd had to fight her way off the street, have said no to the best offer she'd ever had, was ever likely to have? The closest thing to a fairy tale that she could have hoped for?

A girl like her didn't say no, not to something like that. Even if she hadn't really known why he was asking. Even if she'd been scared of falling in love. Even if she'd been determined not to.

And so she'd said it. Simply, sweetly, on something between a sigh and a laugh. 'Yes. *Yes!*'

And Nico had taken her in his arms, and kissed her senseless, and for a few seconds—a whole week, even—it had seemed easy. They'd married in a small civil ceremony in Rome, a couple of his employees as their witnesses. She'd signed a prenuptial agreement and hadn't minded the understandable precaution.

He'd messaged his father and cousin, but she hadn't met them, not till the memorial service. She'd stayed in his flat pretty much for their entire marriage, save for the occasional outing for a coffee. Nico had either worked or taken her to bed, with not much else in between. She hadn't met his family, his friends, anyone. He'd never had to introduce her as his wife.

If any of it had rung alarm bells, Emma hadn't let

it, because she'd wanted the fairy tale to be real, if only for a little while. Deep down she'd always known it would end one day, the way everything ended, because why wouldn't it? Why would a man like Nico—rich, powerful, unbearably attractive—stay married to someone like her? Maybe he'd needed to get her out of his system, slum it for a while before he moved on. Emma had told herself she was under no illusions... but part of her had still hoped.

Then, a week later, he'd left, and, while still at his apartment in Rome, she'd heard from a coldly drawling Antonio about the crash. She couldn't think about him, the way his mouth had pulled down and his dark eyes had tracked her, without her stomach cramping.

'Absolutely no survivors,' he'd said shortly. 'And as you've only been married a week, and Nico was tiring of you anyway...'

She hadn't wanted to believe that last part, and yet she had, because people *always* tired of her. The foster families who hadn't wanted to keep her, who had moved her on because she wasn't lovable enough... even the one that she'd let herself love back.

'Emma? No, absolutely not...'

The certainty in her foster mother's voice, a woman she'd dared to love, who she'd begun to think loved her, rejecting her out of hand, with such certainty. It was a memory she couldn't bear to think about, not even all these years later.

In any case, Antonio had made the situation abundantly clear. 'You are not part of this family, and never will be. I'll give you ten thousand dollars, merely as a gesture of goodwill, with the assurance that you will never come sniffing around here again. Is that clear?'

By that time she'd been desperate to get away, stinging from his contempt, from the knowledge that if he'd been around, it would have been Nico, not Antonio, sending her on her way with such a disdainful expression. And so, as she'd clung to the last remnants of her pride, she'd nodded.

'Yes, absolutely clear,' she'd told him, making herself sound mocking, even though her heart had felt as if it were in pieces.

It wasn't. She wouldn't let it be, because she didn't let herself love anyone, not any more. Not even Nico. Especially not Nico.

And yet where did that leave her—*them*—now?

As exhausted as she'd been earlier, Emma knew she wouldn't be able to sleep until she'd spoken to Nico. She wouldn't rest until she knew what he intended for her, for their baby. And if she decided he couldn't be trusted? That he'd take away her child? Well, she knew how to run—far and fast.

But first she needed to explain everything to Will. She certainly owed him that much.

She reached over and pulled out the plug, watched the water swirl down the drain in rose-scented suds. Then she got out of the tub and wrapped herself in the thickest, fluffiest dressing gown she'd ever seen, combing her fingers through her hair and making good use of the hotel's luxury lotions. With nothing more to distract or delay her, she squared her shoulders, lifted her chin, and headed out of the bathroom.

Her bag was just outside the door, and Emma reached in it for her phone, heading to the privacy of the bedroom to make the dreaded call.

'Emma?' Will answered after the first ring. 'Are you okay? I've been worried—'

'Oh, Will. I'm so sorry.'

'So that man is your husband?'

'I thought he was dead. But…he wasn't.'

'He didn't seem that thrilled to see you,' Will remarked, and Emma let out a trembling laugh.

'No, but…we'll work it out.' At least she would try. She hoped Nico would, too.

'Well, you know I'm here for you,' Will said after a moment, and Emma's eyes stung. Even though she'd only known him a short while, Will was a good friend, and she was grateful for him.

'Thank you,' she whispered.

'You will keep in touch?'

'I'll try.' Right now it felt like the most she could offer.

The call finished, Emma knew there was nothing to keep her from seeking out Nico. The marble floor was cold and slick beneath her bare feet as she walked into the massive living area, a vast open space, looking for him. It took her a few minutes to find him, standing on the wraparound balcony, gazing out at the city lights.

Emma took a deep breath and then slid open the sliding glass and stepped out onto the balcony, the balmy evening air rushing over her skin, heated from the bath.

'Hello, Nico,' she said quietly.

* * *

Nico turned around, jolted by the soft sound of Emma's voice. He'd been so lost in his thoughts he hadn't heard the door slide back, or realised she'd come out here to join him. He glanced at her now, her face flushed from the bath, her hair curling about her shoulders in damp tendrils. The dressing gown enveloped her and yet still offered a tantalising peek of the shadowy vee between her breasts, a hidden valley whose delights he remembered all too well.

The dressing gown stopped just above her knees, and he could see the shapely curve of her golden legs. Everything about her made him ache to touch her, his palms itching with the need. A simple tug and the sash of her dressing gown would fall away; she'd shrug out of it and step towards him, naked and perfect. He'd take her in his arms as he had before...

With an enormous amount of effort, Nico forced the tempting vision away. He could not complicate matters with sex right now. 'Did you have a nice bath?' he asked in his most solicitous tone.

'Yes, it was amazing.' She offered him a small, wry smile that felt like a truce. 'I forgot how easy it was to get used to this kind of living.'

Presumably she hadn't had it, then, in the three and a half months since his alleged death, which had to have been part of the reason she'd gone for this Will. 'What did you do, after the plane crash?' he asked. He realised he was curious. He'd already determined he needed to know more about her, to figure out if he could trust her. Now seemed to be as good a time as any to start finding the answers he needed, assuming she would tell him the truth. He didn't yet know if that was a reasonable assumption to make.

'After your memorial service, you mean?' She let out a sigh as she turned back to the suite. 'Do you mind if we sit down? My feet are absolutely aching.'

'Are they?' He couldn't keep from sounding concerned, and she let out a little laugh as she walked back inside.

'Three-inch heels and pregnancy do not go together, as it turns out.' She sat on one of the sofas, tucking her legs up underneath her. 'What did I do?' she resumed, her expression turning thoughtful, guarded. 'First let me ask you what you did.'

It was clearly a prevarication, but one he decided he was willing to run with. For now. 'I told you, I was in hospital.'

'Yes, but…' She shook her head slowly, her eyes wide and golden. 'I can't get my head around the fact that you survived a plane crash. That must have been…' she blew out a breath '…terrifying.'

'I don't remember it, actually.' He glanced down, finding it weirdly vulnerable to admit even that much. It felt like a deficiency, a weakness, that his brain had these blanks.

Emma drew her brows together as she studied him. 'You don't?'

'No,' he admitted, settling back into the sofa, his hands splayed on his thighs. 'The crash itself is a complete blank. I don't even remember being on the plane, or any of it. The last thing I can remember comprehensively is—' *kissing you goodbye* '—a bit before,' he finished after a second's pause. 'Apparently, it's common for the brain to block out that kind of trauma. Sometimes the memories come back, sometimes they don't.' He smiled a bit crookedly. 'Or so the doctors told me.'

'Oh, Nico.' Her face softened with sympathy and caused a rush of—something—to course through him. A longing, deeper than desire, stirred in him. This woman had touched him in ways he never had been before. At least, he'd convinced himself of that, when he'd been lying in a hospital bed, with the memory of Emma the only thing he could hold onto. Whether it was a mirage or not hadn't mattered, not then.

But it mattered now. Love was most certainly not going to feature in their future at all, not in any shape or form. He'd learned better now. Wised up, thankfully.

'All I remember is waking up in a hospital bed,' he stated matter-of-factly. 'Staring around and having no idea where I was, or even who I was. Everything was a complete blank—just this whiteness. In my head.' He shook his head slowly as the memory of it filtered through him. 'It was terrifying,' he admitted, 'as well as completely disorientating.'

'I can't even imagine,' Emma exclaimed softly. 'How long was that for? When did your memories come back?'

He shrugged, again feeling that flash of vulnerability at admitting his ignorance. 'It's all a blur, frankly, and it didn't happen all at once. Bits and pieces…like pieces of a puzzle, except I didn't know how they fitted together, or what the whole picture was. For a month I was in a coma, and then another month of not knowing who I was, although I had random memories come and go, like flashes of lightning.' He remembered searching his empty mind, the vacuum of his memory, for much-needed clues, snatching at fragments of memory that drifted through his mind like ghosts, hazy and ephemeral.

'Then I started to remember more things—events, people, and as I got stronger I remembered more and more. Eventually I knew enough to contact my cousin, Antonio.' Who had hardly been overjoyed to hear from him, Nico recalled wryly. Had his cousin been hoping to step into his shoes as CEO of Santini Enterprises? Undoubtedly. Nico's return from the dead must have been a disappointment, although Antonio had at least pretended to be pleased.

'Antonio,' Emma repeated. 'You remembered him first, then?'

No, he'd remembered Emma first. Emma, lying in his bed, smiling up at him, her hair in a curly golden halo about her flushed face. Emma, tilting her chin as she gave him that impish smile, making his heart sing. *Emma.* 'Yes, and my father,' he repeated, and now his tone was just as neutral as hers. He'd remembered his father eventually—and the last conversation they'd had, when the man who had raised him had stared at him stonily before turning away in complete and utter dismissal. He would acknowledge Nico in public, but not in private, not as his son. He would never regard him with anything close to affection, and lying in a hospital bed, as the memories had filtered through him like shards of glass, lacerating his shredded conscience and drawing blood, he'd remembered the reason he'd walked away from his family—and into Emma's arms.

'And me?' she asked softly, glancing down. 'You… you must have remembered me?'

Nico looked away, his jaw bunching. He'd meant to deal simply in facts, but the emotions came chasing behind, galloping up on him, taking him by surprise. 'Yes,' he managed tautly. 'I remembered you.'

The silence that poured over them felt like honey, a golden web of memory weaving them together.

Yes, Nico could not keep from thinking, every thought like an ache deep inside him, *I remembered you. I remembered the exact shade of your eyes, how they glint when you laugh. I remembered precisely how you felt in my arms, how your breasts filled my hands. I remembered the squeal of your laughter as I kissed my way down your body, as the laughter became sighs and then gasps… I remembered it all.*

He swallowed hard. Shifted in his seat, and forced his mind onwards, out of the honeyed trap of the past. 'Anyway,' he said, apropos of nothing.

'Have you remembered everything now?' Emma asked, and now she sounded cautious, wary rather than sympathetic. 'Besides being on the plane, I mean? There aren't any more…gaps?'

'No, at least, I don't think there are. I suppose it's hard to know what you can't remember, if you don't remember it.' Sometimes he felt a nagging sensation that he'd forgotten something important, some conversation or piece of information, like a tickle at the back of his brain, but the doctors had assured him that was normal with amnesiac patients. He'd learned, for the most part, to ignore it. To focus on what he did remember…like Emma, until he'd learned she'd been the one to forget him. Maybe he would have been better forgetting, too, except not if there was a baby involved. His baby.

'That all must have been incredibly difficult,' Emma said quietly.

'It was.' He turned to face her again. Her hair was drying in curls, her face still flushed from the bath, and her dressing gown had slipped off one smooth, golden shoulder. She was utterly delectable, and he could not deny how much he wanted her. Still. Now. His heated blood was racing through his veins, his hands itching to touch her. To draw her to him, onto his lap, his lips on hers, his hands…and they could both forget everything that had happened since then; to catapult back to when it had been easy, the two of them in bed, making each other's bodies sing.

He took a steadying breath. 'Tell me your side of the story, Emma. What happened after you learned I had died? What did you do?'

The soft look of compassion on her face fell away in an instant, replaced by something far more guarded. 'I went to LA,' she said after a moment. 'As you know.'

'Yes, but why?' He leaned forward, wondering if this, perhaps, was the nub of it, the thing he didn't understand, or maybe he just didn't want to understand. Didn't want to accept she was exactly what Antonio had said she was from the beginning—only in it for the money. 'My family would have provided for you, you know, as my wife. I know we hadn't been married long, but—'

'No, they wouldn't have.' She cut across him, the words quiet and so very sure. 'As it happened, they didn't. They refused, not that I even asked, because it was obvious enough already.'

Nico frowned. 'Antonio said he offered you ten thousand dollars—'

'Yes, that's true, as a gesture of his goodwill.' Her mouth twisted as she made air quotes with her hands. 'Which I took, because I didn't have so much as a penny to my name, and I was desperate. I'm not ashamed to admit that.' Up went her chin, along with the golden flash of her eyes. 'But there was no suggestion of me staying with your family, Nico.' She paused, as if she were going to say something more, and then decided not to. 'I can't really begrudge your cousin or father that, though, considering the circumstances. You'd only known me a month. Antonio didn't know me at all. And I did take the money he offered, so I suppose he thought that proved whatever it was he thought about me.'

Nico stared at her in dismayed surprise, because this was definitely not how his cousin had framed the events. Antonio had insisted Emma had wanted to leave, had demanded the money he'd reluctantly given, and then gone on her merry way, shaking the dust from her shoes. Who was he to believe?

Looking at the lines of bitter hurt etched into Emma's face, he felt compelled to believe her version, even as he resisted such a notion, because what did it say about his cousin? His family? And yet should he really be surprised, considering how hard-nosed his father had been? How cynical his cousin? 'Antonio said you couldn't wait to leave,' he said slowly.

'That much is true,' she admitted. She glanced away, as if to hide her expression. 'I knew I wasn't wanted, so I chose to leave.'

He sat back, his mind whirling, his stomach tightening. This was definitely not the story he'd been sold, although he realised he wasn't really surprised. Why would his father be interested in his wife, when he hadn't been interested in *him*? And Antonio had always been pragmatic to the point of ruthlessness. Nico could still recall the way Antonio had grimaced when he'd told him he was marrying her.

'Keep her as your mistress, for heaven's sake, Nico, but don't actually marry the girl!'

And Nico, in a fit of pique, and a deeper hurt at the widening fissure between him and his cousin, had ignored that advice. Maybe he shouldn't have, he acknowledged grimly, but it was too late now. But why had he let himself believe Antonio's version of events upon his return? Was it because he'd been so wounded by Emma's apparent betrayal, by marrying again? Anger always felt like the stronger option.

'Do you believe me?' Emma asked, a vulnerable note creeping into her voice, making him ache.

'Yes,' he admitted, shaken by the truth of his words—and hers. 'I do.'

Suddenly the last three months—three and a half—took on a whole new, uncomfortable complexion. If Emma had left his family, knowing she wasn't welcomed…if she'd discovered she was pregnant with so very few resources…and if Will had offered to marry and provide for her…why wouldn't she say yes? For the sake of her—their—child?

Was it really fair to judge her for any of that? To be angry about it?

'Nico?' Emma asked softly, breaking into his thoughts. 'What are you thinking?'

I'm thinking that I wish things were simple and straightforward, but they never are. I want to trust you even now, but I won't let myself because I've had to learn not to trust people.

His mother, who had lied to him his whole life. His father, who had rejected him. Antonio, the cousin who had been like a brother, until he'd discovered he wasn't. No, he wasn't about to be that honest, not with Emma, not with anyone. 'I'm sorry you had to face that,' he said, his voice roughening to hide his emotion. 'That would not have been my intention…or my wish, for you to have been cast out in such a way without any resources, financial or otherwise.'

She shrugged, glancing down as a tendril of her golden-brown hair fell in front of her face, obscuring her expression. 'I don't blame your cousin for that, to be honest. He barely knew me. *You* barely knew me.' She looked up then, and Nico was taken aback by the challenge in her eyes.

No, he realised, he hadn't really known her, but he'd thought he had. Was that his fault? For being so willing to believe, to jump with both feet, simply because he'd wanted to, so much, in a moment of weakness and wanting, when his own father had turned away from him?

'Still,' he said, 'it must have been very difficult for you.'

She shrugged, managed one of her old, insouciant smiles that still had the power to lighten his heart, even though he saw it didn't reach her eyes. 'Hey, ten grand is ten grand. It bought me an economy-class ticket to LA, and two months' food and rent until I found a job, got on my feet.'

And that was presumably when she'd run out of options—and met Will. It was all starting to make a terrible sort of sense. And, Nico realised, he was starting to believe—and even trust—his wife, at least in terms of this part of her story. Or at least want to, he supposed.

His heart, he knew, was another matter entirely.

CHAPTER SEVEN

EMMA SNUGGLED DEEPER under the covers, sleepily enjoying the luxuriously smooth feel of the silken sheets, the comfortingly heavy duvet. Her bones felt as if they were melting into the soft mattress, every muscle wonderfully relaxed for the first time in ages. Her eyes closed, her mind in a pleasant haze of sleep, she stretched like a starfish—and encountered a hard chest. A hard, warm, very *male* chest, muscles tensing and flexing under her questing palm.

She should have jerked her hand away. Even in her sleep-hazed state, some part of her knew this, absolutely. For her own health and safety, her own *sanity*, not to mention her battered heart, she should yank her hand back, jump out of bed and keep things very, very clear, at least in *that* regard. But in her sleepily befuddled state, she didn't. For a second, no more, she flattened her palm against that hair-roughened chest, enjoying the tickle of the crisp hairs underneath her palm, the flexing muscles, the warm, burnished skin.

Then a strong male hand captured her own, whether to still it or simply keep it there, she didn't know. Her breath caught in her chest and although she was still asleep—*mostly*—she moved out of instinct, out of need, unable to think past the blooming warmth and want deep in her belly. She rolled right into all that potent male warmth next to her in the bed, letting it engulf her, swallow her whole. At least that was what it felt like, as if she were being wonderfully subsumed.

In the next moment, the hand that had held her own had moved to the dip of her waist, slipping under her T-shirt and spanning her warm, welcoming flesh, covering it, owning it. Her hips came into contact with the very male part of Nico, nestling perfectly against him and sending a shockwave of sensation buzzing through her. *Now* she was awake. Very awake.

And now her mind was in an entirely different sort of haze—one of overwhelming, intoxicating desire. It thudded through her, made every sense blaze and yearn and strive, consequences be damned. Without being able to stop herself, not even wanting to, she pressed into him, sending fiery arrows of pleasure sizzling through her as his arousal pulsed between her thighs. Nico let out a muttered groan and, with his hands on her waist, he fastened her hips more securely against his, pressing against her, into her, so need flared deeper, hotter as his mouth captured her own in a plundering kiss and she remembered just how explosive it had been between them. How completely wonderful, shocking in its intensity, exciting in its passion, overwhelming her with both.

His touch was a tornado that caught her up in its heady whirl, as his mouth ravaged her own with a tender, velvety persistence and her mind blurred with longing. She grabbed his shoulders, anchoring herself to him as his hand slid from her waist to between her thighs, touching her with such clever, knowing intimacy that had her gasping aloud, pressing into him, yearning for more. She'd forgotten how good this was between them, how he made her come alive in a way she never, ever had before.

And Nico must have felt just as much as she did, for his breathing was ragged and fast as he fumbled with the overlarge T-shirt she'd worn as pyjamas, desperate to press his heated flesh against hers, just as Emma was...

Yet somehow, in the blur of desire, the blaze of need, sanity asserted itself, that still, small voice telling her this was really *not* a good idea, all things considered. Somehow she managed to hold onto that faintest shred of common sense even though everything in her was longing for more. So much more.

'*Wait.*' Emma pushed at his chest, which felt like an immovable wall, and to his credit Nico stilled instantly, his body pressed to hers, his *hand*...

'Emma?' His voice came out in a throaty rasp, his lips inches from hers, his forehead sheened with sweat as he held himself back.

'We shouldn't...' She hitched her breath as longing coursed through her. *Be smart, Emma. Stay safe.* 'I'm sorry, but I'm not... I'm not ready for this.'

Even if right in this moment she felt ready, more than ready. She was *yearning*. But if she gave herself to him, Emma knew, she'd lose her focus to stay strong. Smart. Safe. She might even lose herself.

She needed to figure out what their future was, before she let him into her bed, because as smart as she was trying to be, it was only a hop, skip and a jump from bed to heart, and she was not going to make that leap. Not now, and maybe not ever. She'd told herself she could separate the two before, and she might do it again, but right now she felt too vulnerable to even attempt to make that division.

Slowly Nico withdrew from her, and it felt like a loss. 'I apologise,' he said stiffly as he rolled up into a seated position, driving his fingers through his dark hair as a shuddery breath went through him.

'You don't need to…' she began helplessly, and then, not really knowing how to finish that sentence, she pressed back against the pillows and closed her eyes. Her heart was thudding, her body tingling everywhere with awakened, unanswered desire. Was she being really stupid? It wasn't as if they hadn't slept together before. Playing the prude when she was pregnant with his baby was kind of ridiculous, wasn't it?

And yet…she felt vulnerable enough already, and that was an emotion she didn't like. She wasn't about to become even more so.

'I'm the one who should be sorry,' she whispered. 'I didn't mean to…well, it all just sort of happened, I guess.'

'Well, I know it.'

He sounded wry, and Emma cracked open an eye, surprised he wasn't doing the whole coldly furious thing with her. He smiled down at her, definitely looking rueful, colour slashing his cheeks, his green eyes glinting, and she found herself smiling back. A laugh escaped her like a bubble, the last thing she expected right now, but she was glad for it. This side of Nico, playful and wry, was so much nicer than the arrogant, autocratic man she'd encountered last night. She was glad for it, for him.

'Come on,' he said, hauling her up by the hand. 'We have a doctor's appointment this morning.'

'We do?' Last night, after their conversation, she'd crashed into bed, too exhausted to as much as stir when Nico had obviously come in to sleep on the other side. She hadn't been aware he was there until morning, when she'd stretched and come into contact with him, in all his male glory.

'Yes, I arranged it last night, after you went to bed, with an obstetrician.'

He rose from the bed, wearing nothing but a pair of navy silk boxer shorts, looking utterly magnificent, his skin like burnished satin over bunched muscle, making her long to touch him again. Slide her hand along that warm, satiny skin.

Stop it, Emma.

'I had a scan two weeks ago,' she told him. 'Everything was fine with the baby then. I don't think I need another—'

'Well, I want to see for myself,' Nico replied, his tone firm as he headed towards the bathroom. 'And then, of course, there's the matter of a paternity test.'

Oh. Emma stared at his retreating back, watched as he closed the bathroom door with a firm click. Right, a paternity test. Because he still didn't trust that he was the father. Still thought she might be lying to his face, and about something so important.

Well, maybe stopping things before they got out of hand *had* been a good idea, then. She told herself she shouldn't feel hurt that Nico was being thorough; after all, they'd known each other for such a short time, and raising a child was a big deal. She told herself that, but Emma knew it didn't make much difference. She *was* hurt, and she was annoyed at herself for being so.

A lifetime of living on the sidelines of other people's lives had taught her not to care, and definitely not to love or try to be loved. That had never worked out, starting with her mother, from whom she'd been taken away when she was just six months old, and then following with the foster families she'd tried so desperately to belong to. Some had been kind, some not so much, some downright cruel, but not one of them had ever actually *wanted* her. Chosen her, even the one she thought might. The one she'd let herself love.

Emma? Absolutely not.

She'd never forget those words, that tone, spoken over the phone by the foster mum she'd come to love, when she'd thought she wasn't listening. She had been, in hope, knowing the social worker would be calling, thinking her foster mum might finally say the words she'd been waiting to hear her whole life.

Emma. Yes. Of course.

After that she'd made the decision, at ten years old, not to let anybody in ever again. It had been a conscious choice, one she'd always stood by.

Work hard, act tough, be funny, make like you don't care and then you won't.

She could not let Nico Santini get under those defences...even if she was married to him. She'd resolved it before, and she would do so again.

Yes, it was a very good thing things hadn't progressed farther this morning. And they wouldn't do so again, not until she'd figured out how she was going to navigate this whole situation. Unfortunately a restful night's sleep had not presented her with a solution. The fact remained she was still married to Nico, pregnant with his child, and unsure what their living situation could possibly look like.

The bathroom door opened, and Nico strode out, a towel slung low around his hips, his hair damp and spiky from the shower.

Emma watched, her mouth drying, as he reached for a pair of boxers from the suitcase open on a luggage rack. He dropped the towel and she hastily averted her eyes.

'Nico,' she protested weakly.

'What?' He sounded utterly unrepentant as he slid on a pair of boxers. Yes, she'd peeked from the corner of her eye, unable to resist the sight of the fabric sliding over his taut, muscled flesh. 'It's not as if you haven't seen it before, and we *are* married.'

A far cry from the man who had said they would divorce just yesterday. How could she possibly trust him—not just with her own life, but with that of their child? 'We might be married but not like that,' Emma replied, determined not to let him befuddle her with his body.

'Almost like that,' Nico replied, his voice lowering to a silken purr, making her blush. 'Very almost, as of this morning.' He reached for a crisp blue shirt from the wardrobe and slid his arms into it.

'Yes, about that,' Emma said, hugging her knees to

her chest. 'I thought you'd sleep on the sofa or some-thing.'

'The sofas aren't that comfortable, and besides, the bed was plenty big enough.' He turned around to face her, his long, lean fingers buttoning up the shirt, hid-ing his magnificent chest. The chest she remembered exploring with her fingertips just moments earlier.

'Not that big,' Emma pointed out. 'Seriously, Nico… we have to come to some sort of agreement, about what happens now.'

'What happens now?' His eyebrows rose as he straightened the cuffs of his shirt. 'It seems quite simple to me. You're my wife, I'm your husband, and that—' he nodded towards her middle '—is our baby.'

'You didn't seem so sure about that when you booked a paternity test this morning,' Emma retorted, and Nico looked startled.

'Emma, be reasonable. I have to be sure.'

Yes, because he couldn't trust her.

And you can't trust him.

And what was a marriage without trust? What was a *family*?

'Emma, surely you can see that?' he pressed, his voice so very reasonable.

Yes, she thought reluctantly, she supposed she could, all things considered, and yet it still stung, a *lot*, and it made her wonder how on earth this mar-riage of theirs was ever supposed to work, on any level. What did Nico even want—for her to fall in with his plans, pop out his baby, warm his bed?

Would that even be so bad?

Emma had always been a pragmatist; she'd had to

be. Nico would always provide for her, she knew, and she could finally live without fear of where her next meal was coming from, or whether there would be a roof over her head. She'd never wanted to be loved, had chosen not to, and yet…

What if he walked away from their child, the way her mother had walked away from her? Could she subject her baby to such a risk?

Did she have a choice?

Nico couldn't tell what was bothering Emma, at least not exactly. He eyed her as they rode to the appointment he'd booked at one of the city's most exclusive obstetrics clinics in Beverly Hills, noting her narrowed eyes and pursed lips, the way she angled her head away from him. She'd been prickly since they'd woken up this morning…and what a way to wake up!

Was what had happened in bed between them this morning annoying her? As exciting as that delicious little interlude had been, it had also been unexpected, both of them caught up in the throes of their passion before they'd so much as blinked the sleep from their eyes. Not that he'd minded. At all. But, he acknowledged, it wasn't something they had discussed or planned, and maybe Emma hadn't been ready for it.

Or, he wondered, was it the fact he'd made this appointment? She'd seemed surprised and maybe even a little annoyed that he'd made it in the first place. Yet surely Emma could see the unfortunate necessity of a paternity test? It wasn't meant to be an insult on her character, simply a sensible precaution. Although, he realised uncomfortably, he supposed it *could* seem as though he didn't trust her.

Yet how was he meant to trust her when he'd walked in on her wedding to another man? Besides, considering his own parentage, he knew he needed to be absolutely certain that he was this baby's father. The test, he knew, was as much about him as it was about her...not that he intended to explain to her about that.

In any case, he decided, he'd get to the bottom of it after the doctor's appointment. Lay it all on the table, make everything clear. And tell her exactly what he expected from their marriage.

He glanced at her again, noticing the way she held herself, as if she were all sharp angles and edges, her expression both resolute and resigned. Nico found he didn't like her looking like that. He liked seeing her laugh, giving as good as she got, but since he'd told her they were going to the doctor's, all he'd got from her were monosyllables.

Last night—and this morning—had clarified things for him. Assuming the baby was his—and maybe even if it wasn't—he knew now he wanted a proper marriage with Emma. They had too much chemistry to ignore, and even when she was infuriating him, she made him smile. He enjoyed her company and he genuinely liked her. All good reasons, he thought, for her to be a proper wife, and for them to be a proper family. This time he wouldn't entertain fantastical notions of love, but he would enjoy all the other benefits of their union—from their time in bed to being a father.

As for Emma...she would have the same enjoyments. Surely she couldn't argue against that? She'd

been willing to marry that mopey software engineer
for money, why not him? He was, Nico reflected,
offering a *much* better deal. So why was she looking
so annoyed right now?

Perhaps, he mused, he needed to be clearer what
he was offering. How much. She'd only had a taste
of the wealth and luxury at his disposal before the
crash; now he would give her the full measure of it.
He'd enjoy pampering her, he realised. Although she'd
been sparing with the details of her childhood, she'd
made it clear that she had no family, and her circumstances when he'd met her had seemed dire indeed.
He'd enjoyed pampering her before, and he would do
so even more now. He looked forward to giving her
all the things she hadn't had before—travel, clothes,
jewellery, evenings out…really, she had it made. She
just didn't realise it yet. He couldn't wait to tell her.

The obstetrician's clinic was just a short ride away, off
Rodeo Drive, a discreet brick building with a gold-
plated plaque. Nico kept his hand on the small of her
back as he ushered her into the comfortable waiting
room, and gave their names to the receptionist at the
front desk. Glancing at Emma, he saw how closed and
pinched her expression was, her arms folded across
her middle as she seemed to be doing her damnedest
not to meet his eye.

Within a few minutes they were called, and Nico
accompanied her into the examining room, as much
to support her as to hear the information himself. The
obstetrician, a kindly faced woman with curly grey

hair, smiled at them both, a slight query in her brown eyes as she looked between them.

'Signora Santini?' she asked, looking directly at Emma. 'How can I help you today?'

Emma shot Nico an uncertain glance before replying in a half-mumble, 'I just need a check-up, I suppose.'

'Of course.'

'And a paternity test,' Nico filled in, only to feel as if the temperature in the room had taken a sudden nose-dive. Emma was staring down at her lap and the obstetrician was giving him a coldly bland look.

'I see,' she said.

'That is possible, is it not?' Nico pressed. 'The receptionist assured me—'

'It is possible,' the obstetrician agreed, in a tone that matched her decidedly cool expression. 'Now, if you don't mind, I will examine Signora Santini in private.'

'But—'

The obstetrician pointed to the door. 'You can wait outside. Thank you, *signor.*'

Nico stared at her, flummoxed, before realising he had no choice but to exit the examining room.

'Very well,' he said, and with a glance at Emma, who seemed determined not to look at him, he left the room.

Outside he paced the waiting room, unable to stand still, wondering why he'd been excluded from the appointment, and fuming that he had. The whole point of this exercise had been to be more involved, not less. To build trust. Instead he'd been shown the door as if he shouldn't have been there in the first place.

Loyal Readers
FREE BOOKS Voucher

We're giving away **THOUSANDS** of **FREE** **BOOKS**

Don't Miss Out! Send for Your Free Books Today!

See Details Inside

Get up to 4
FREE FABULOUS BOOKS
You Love!

To thank you for being a loyal reader we'd like to send you up to 4 FREE BOOKS, absolutely free when you try the Harlequin Reader Service.

Just write "YES" on the Loyal Reader Voucher and we'll send you 2 free books from each series you choose and a Free Mystery Gift, altogether worth over $20.

Try **Harlequin® Desire** and get 2 books featuring the worlds of the American elite with juicy plot twists, delicious sensuality and intriguin scandal.

Try **Harlequin Presents® Larger-Print** and get 2 books featuring the glamourous lives of royals and billionaires in a world of exotic locations, where passion knows no bounds.

Or **TRY BOTH** and get 2 books from each series!

Your free books are completely free, even the shipping! If you continue with your subscription, you can look forward to curated monthly shipments of brand-new books from your selected series, always at a discount off the cover price! Plus you can cancel any time.

So don't miss out, return your Loyal Readers Voucher today to get your Free books.

Pam Powers

LOYAL READER
FREE BOOKS VOUCHER

And all right, he understood that this was women's stuff, and maybe Emma would like some privacy if the OB was going to poke and prod. But he still didn't like being cut out, and it left him feeling distinctly edgy and irritable to be kept in the dark. Neither sensation abated when, half an hour later, Emma emerged from the office, pale-faced but composed, and still not looking at him.

'Well?' he asked, and she just gave a little shrug, folding her arms and looking away.

'The results of the tests will be available tomorrow,' the OB told him in that same cool voice she'd used before. 'Emma has agreed to share any medical information with you, so I'll email a full work-up of her blood tests, in addition to the matter of paternity.'

He supposed he should be satisfied with that, but he was still left with the feeling he'd done something wrong. 'Thank you,' Nico bit out, and then, taking Emma's arm, he ushered her outside to the waiting car.

CHAPTER EIGHT

WELL, THAT HAD been absolutely humiliating, on far too many fronts. Emma scooted to the far side of the car as Nico slid in next to her. She turned her face to the window, unable to bear even looking at him. She was trying not to feel so hurt, heaven knew, but it was hard. Very hard.

'I've booked The Ivy for lunch,' Nico informed her as the driver closed the door and they started off.

'I'd rather not,' Emma squeezed out through a throat that felt too tight. 'I'd rather just return to the hotel.'

'You need to eat.'

Which was true enough, as the obstetrician had told her, among other things, that she was more than a bit underweight. Emma had explained about the morning sickness, and the doctor had been sympathetic, but also stern, more so than the doctor at the free clinic she'd gone to before, who had barely looked at her medical files.

'Think about the baby,' she'd told her, and Emma had, for a few seconds, felt like bursting into either tears or hysterical laughter.

I am, she'd wanted to say. *Trust me, I am.*

'I'll get room service, then,' she said. 'And you can watch me eat it, if you're so worried. But I don't need to swank about The Ivy.'

'Swank about? Is that what we'd be doing?' Nico sounded caught between amusement and annoyance.

'Whatever.' She hunched a shoulder, keeping her gaze away from him.

'I also thought we could do some shopping,' Nico remarked mildly. 'For some new clothes. You only had a few things in your suitcase, and they did not seem entirely suitable.'

'I only had a few things, period.' He'd arranged to have her things brought from Will's last night, and, going through them, Emma had realised just how shabby they were—a couple of pairs of jeans and some T-shirts. She hadn't wanted to ask Will to pay for anything before they were married.

'What happened to the things I bought you?' Nico asked, his voice mild, yet with an undercurrent of steel. Before his accident, he'd taken her shopping in Rome, and she'd cautiously picked out a few things, hardly daring to believe he'd let her, not wanting to press her luck.

'I left them in Rome,' she told him, her gaze still on the window. 'There wasn't the opportunity to take them with me.'

'You mean because of Antonio?' Nico asked, and now his voice held a thrum of anger, although this time not for her, thankfully. She hoped, anyway.

'Pretty much,' Emma replied shortly. 'He showed me the door and didn't give me the option of going back for anything, so I didn't.'

'I'm sorry about that,' Nico said after a moment, his voice terse. 'But surely there's all the more reason to shop for new, then,' he added. He had the deliberately mild voice of someone who was determined to be patient but finding it trying. Well, her patience had been tried all morning. Excessively.

'Maybe later,' she forced out. 'No need to buy me clothes if the baby's not yours, after all, and we won't find that out until tomorrow.' She turned to him and bared her teeth in a saccharine smile. 'Best to wait, don't you think?'

Nico's breath came out in a rush as his eyes narrowed. 'Is *that* why you're in a snit...?'

Emma stiffened. 'I'm not in a *snit.*'

'Annoyed, then. In a mood. Whatever.' His words came out in short, sharp bursts. 'I told you, the paternity test was simply a precaution. The test results will be returned within twenty-four hours, and in the meantime—'

'Fine, then. Like I said, I can wait till then for some new clothes.' She turned back to the window, more so Nico couldn't see the tears that had stupidly sprung to her eyes.

'Emma—'

'I mean it, Nico.' She didn't think she could take any more of this pointless arguing, not when she felt so raw. So *flayed.* Everything about that appointment had been excruciating, from having Nico demand the paternity test, to the OB asking her all sorts of personal questions, including ones about the more difficult aspects of her childhood spent in care, making her feel like some sort of pathetic freak. The last thing she wanted to do was dine and shop like the gold-digger Nico still seemed to think she was. 'Please just take me back to the hotel.'

'Fine.' He rapped on the glass that separated them from the driver and then issued terse instructions to return to the hotel. They didn't speak for the rest of the journey.

Emma was out of the door as soon as the car had pulled up to the kerb, and she marched towards the hotel without waiting for Nico to catch up with her. All she wanted was to barricade herself in the bedroom, or wherever she could find some modicum of privacy. Unfortunately, he had the key card to work the lift, so she had to stand in front of the doors, silently fuming, while she waited for him to stroll up.

'This tantrum of yours is most unbecoming,' he remarked, and she swung around, fists bunched, ready to punch him—or maybe burst into tears.

'My *tantrum*? Haven't you insulted me enough for one day? Or do you have some kind of quota you have to fill?' Unfortunately the words of angry challenge were belied by the catch in her voice. Emma saw Nico's expression change from irritation to confusion before she looked away, blinking as fast as she could to keep the tears at bay. Stupid, *stupid* pregnancy hormones. That was all this had to be, because normally she was so much tougher than this. She'd had to be.

The lift door opened and Emma marched inside, turning away from Nico. He remained silent as the lift soared upwards, the seconds ticking onward endlessly. Did it normally take this long? Eighteen floors wasn't *that* many.

Then, finally, the doors opened and Emma hurried into the penthouse, ready to barricade herself in the bathroom, or wherever she could get the space to cry in private, because she realised that was what she was going to do, whether she wanted to or not. The tears were coming, blinking be damned, and she was afraid it wasn't just because of hormones.

'Emma.' Nico's voice was quiet. Gentle, which didn't help. Now she was really going to blub.

'Please,' she whispered, and found she couldn't manage any more.

'Please tell me what's going on,' he stated quietly. 'I've upset you, I realise, and I want to know why.'

'If you don't know why, then you're an idiot,' she retorted, her voice muffled with the effort of holding back her tears. One slipped down her cheek and she dashed it away as discreetly as she could.

'Then I'm an idiot. Let's talk this through, please.' Although his tone was still gentle, it was one that didn't brook argument. Autocratic even in this. Although, Emma realised, she didn't even want to argue, at least not entirely. In twenty-four hours, Nico was going to discover he was the father of her baby, which meant he was either going to want to stay married, at least in some shape or form, or demand custodial rights and do what she feared most—take her baby away from her.

She had to make sure they worked things out, for better or worse, for the sake of their child.

'Fine.' She dropped her bag onto a chair by the lift doors and then walked to one of the leather sofas and curled up in the corner, letting her hair swing down to hide her face. She needed *some* kind of armour. 'Let's talk.'

Nico stared at her for a moment. 'First, I'll order some food. You need to eat.'

'So you're always telling me.' She waited for him to make the call, but he handed her the menu first.

'What would you like?'

'You're not going to tell me what the best thing on the menu is?' she retorted, before she could rein in her temper. Now was not the time to score petty points, but maybe that was all part of it. His arrogance. His authority. For a month, when she'd felt as if she'd fallen into a fairy tale, it had been more or less okay. But for the rest of her life? *For her baby's life?*

'I think you can decide for yourself what you want to eat.' The smile he gave her was wry, and it calmed her a bit, because it showed he was learning, if just a little. He could change, at least in this small way, or at least act as if he could change. It was small comfort, but it *was* still comfort, and she'd take that where she could find it.

'I'll have the soup and salad, please.' She handed him back the menu and he made the call, ordering a steak and salad for himself. With that out of the way, there was nothing for them to do but stare at each other and wait for one or the other to begin.

Nico sat on the sofa opposite her, loose-limbed and attentive, his green gaze steady on her. Even now she couldn't help but marvel at how breathtakingly attractive he was. That jaw. Those eyes. The hooded brows, the dark hair, the smell of his aftershave...

Focus, Emma.

'All right,' Nico said. 'Now, will you please tell me what has upset you?'

Emma took a deep breath and let it out slowly. She angled her head up to stare at the ceiling because looking at him suddenly felt too hard, and it might keep the tears from slipping down her cheeks. They were definitely pooling in her eyes, so blinking was clearly not an option.

'Nico, do you have any idea,' she began slowly, 'can you even imagine, how absolutely humiliating it is for the father of your baby to inform an obstetrician that he's there for a paternity test? *He* is, clearly not both of you, because he is the only one with the doubts about who you slept with. And then to face a whole bunch of questions after you'd left the room, to make sure I hadn't been coerced into the marriage, or was being abused, or anything like that.'

As well as questions she wasn't going to tell him about, about how she'd been treated as a child, why she had signs of malnutrition, of broken bones that hadn't been healed. Emma had explained as quickly as she could about being in care, about how some families weren't as nice as others.

And even the nice ones let you down.

'Well?' Emma asked when Nico was silent for a long moment. She couldn't risk taking her gaze from the ceiling, although she realised she was curious— and more than a little apprehensive—to know what his expression was. The silence felt ominous the longer it ticked on. What was he thinking, and, if she dared to look at him, would she be able to tell from those hooded eyes, that still face?

'Framed like that,' he answered at last, his voice low and level, 'it seems like it would be more humiliating for me than for you. Or at least more revealing. I'm not exactly thrilled that the OB thought I might be some kind of abuser.'

Emma let out a huff of humourless laughter. 'Yet I'm the one who had to answer all those questions, and who felt like some—some *floozy* who has lost track of the men she's slept with.' Among other things. The pity in the doctor's eyes when she'd explained about her childhood still made her cringe.

'Emma, you're not some *floozy*. I know that.'

'Then why did you insist on the test?' She lowered her gaze to look at him, anger thankfully taking the place of hurt, so the tears didn't fall.

He hesitated, before answering carefully, 'Considering I walked into your wedding, is it not at least a little understandable why I might need some tangible proof?'

She blew out a breath. 'I explained about Will and me,' she reminded him, trying to sound as reasonable as he was. 'How we were friends. I didn't have a ton of options, you know, Nico—'

'I do know that.' A weary sigh escaped him as he rubbed a hand over his face. 'Emma, trust me, I do know. At least, I understand. I had no idea my cousin acted the way he did until you told me about it, and he certainly didn't give that impression to me, but I believe you. I'm… I'm not judging you, for wanting to marry Will, all things considered.'

Her eyebrows arched as she stared at him in disbelief. 'Really? Because you certainly seemed to be right up until this very—'

'I apologise.' He spoke stiffly as he dropped his hand from his face. Now he didn't look angry or annoyed, but weary. Vulnerable, even, although Emma tried to steel herself against feeling too much sympathy. Softer emotions were not for her, pregnancy hormones or not. 'The truth is,' Nico said, his voice a low rumble, 'this paternity test was as much about me, as it was about you, if not…if not more so.'

'What?' Emma stared at him blankly. She had no idea what that was supposed to mean.

'I felt that I have to be absolutely sure I'm the father of this baby,' he continued, 'because…' He paused, took a breath, and then continued resolutely, 'Because my father wasn't sure about me.'

Emma gaped at him, shocked into silence. She had not been expecting *that*. 'What…?' she finally said, not even sure what question she was trying to ask.

'My father questioned my paternity,' Nico explained tonelessly, not quite looking at her. 'Although I only discovered that recently. He learned that he wasn't actually my biological father fairly recently, as well, but as I said he always had his suspicions…and he made it known, in his own way, all through my childhood.'

Nico glanced away from the stunned look on Emma's face, wishing he hadn't admitted so much, and yet knowing he'd had to, for her sake. He couldn't let her go on believing this had simply been about him not trusting her. It was himself he didn't trust, if she could ever even understand that. He might have masked it as a distrust of her, it was true, but at its root this was about him. His vulnerability and insecurity, something he'd never wanted to admit to her, to anyone, yet for her sake he had to.

'I didn't know that,' Emma said quietly, and somehow Nico managed to dredge up a wry smile.

'I know you didn't, because I never told you before.'

'I suppose,' she said slowly, 'there are a lot of things we don't know about each other.'

'We only knew each other a month,' he agreed, which was another reason for the paternity test, although not nearly as pressing as the doubts that clamoured inside himself. He never wanted his own child to feel the way he had. He never wanted to have the doubts his father had had, although he hoped he would be a better man and not show it the way his father had, in a thousand tiny, cutting ways, over and over again through the years.

'Why…?' Emma asked slowly 'Why did your father have such doubts about you?'

'Because my mother had an affair around the time I was conceived.' He swallowed hard, fighting the urge to shift in his seat, because none of this was easy. Saying it all aloud brought back all of the painful memories, made him remember just how much they had hurt. His mother's halting admission, on her deathbed, so he'd felt as if he were losing her in more ways than one. How she'd always suspected but never told him, never helped him to understand why his father had been cold to him his whole life. He remembered his father's icily disdainful expression, his utter refusal to be moved. 'I didn't know about it until recently, as it happened,' he told Emma. 'I believe I told you my mother had died shortly before I met you?'

'Yes, a few months before.' Emma's face was already softening in sympathy, and Nico found he had to look away.

'She told me on her deathbed,' he forced out. 'She wanted to make it right somehow, but in some ways, I wish she'd never said a word, or maybe she'd told me a lot sooner, to help me to understand. I confronted my father, who admitted he had always had his doubts. I insisted we have a paternity test done as soon as possible, and so we did.' He swallowed. 'The results were conclusive. I was the product of an affair.'

He struggled not to close his eyes against the onslaught of that painful memory—his father's hardened expression, the way he'd turned away, dismissing him utterly. *I've always known, really.*

'Oh, Nico.' The gentle sorrow in her voice was nearly his undoing. 'I'm so sorry.'

He shrugged. 'In the end, it didn't change very much. Considering the situation, I offered to step aside as CEO of Santini Enterprises. Antonio is his blood relation and he would be just as good at the job, and I have my own business interests as it is. It seemed logical, but my father refused.' He let out a long, low breath. 'He said he didn't want to encourage speculation, which would be humiliating for him.' It had always, Nico had realised then, been about his father's pride. Not about him. Not even about Antonio, who had fumed at being passed over.

'And your relationship?' Emma asked after a moment. 'With your father? Did that…?'

Nico shrugged. 'It is what it is, what it has always been. Distant to the point of being non-existent, if I'm perfectly honest.' He paused, wondering whether to admit more, then deciding Emma deserved it. 'I tried to win his love when I was younger, did everything I could, but none of it was ever enough.' Getting good grades, always on his best behaviour, waiting by the window for his father to come home…and then later, as an adult, working all hours God gave him to prove himself, without ever understanding that it was a Sisyphean task. That he would never, ever be able to prove himself to his father. 'I stopped a long time ago,' he told Emma, although it hadn't been long enough. And even when he'd stopped trying, the feeling had persisted—that he wasn't good enough, he wasn't worthy of love. No, he wasn't about to make those kinds of admissions to Emma right now. There was being honest, and then there was being stupid. Pathetic.

He'd told himself that at least he now knew why his father had always acted as if he didn't love him. Surely that was better than always wondering, always trying and failing, again and again.

'And your cousin?' Emma asked after a moment, her tone turning probing yet cautious. 'What about your relationship with him?'

Nico shrugged. 'We were close when we were younger, as we're both only children, and we were raised almost as brothers. Antonio is my father's sister's son, and she died when he was a teenager, so he came into our family.' And his father loved Antonio more than he loved him, Nico knew. Antonio had Santini blood in his veins while he did not. Something else that shouldn't hurt any more, all things considered, but it did. 'Later, though, we grew apart, and more so when my paternity was revealed. Antonio wanted to step in as CEO, and my father refused.'

He turned to Emma, who was frowning, seeming lost in thought, her arms wrapped around her knees. 'Why are you asking?' he asked, because she was looking strangely hesitant and uncertain, as if she wanted to say more but wasn't sure she dared. In response to his question, she only nibbled her lip. Didn't speak. Unease deepened inside him, churning his gut. 'Emma?'

'It's…' She hesitated, and Nico had that tickling sensation he'd had before, at the back of his brain, when he'd been trying to remember something that had been eluding him. Was it about Emma? *Emma and Antonio?* But she'd only met him after his alleged death, and Antonio had sent her off. Hadn't he? Why was his mind spiralling out of control, into suspicion? What had he forgotten?

No, he needed to stop jumping to conclusions, fearing the worst because it had happened with his father. Not everyone was so untrustworthy, so unloving, and yet Emma…

Could he really trust her?

'Emma, what is it?' he demanded roughly.

A sigh escaped and she rested her forehead on her knees. Nico felt as if his stomach were suddenly coated in ice, his lungs frozen so it hurt to breathe. What on earth was she finding it so difficult to tell him? What more could there be?

'It's about Antonio,' she said at last. 'Something he said.'

'Something he said? What can you possibly mean? What happened between you and Antonio?' His tone came out cold, to hide his fear, and Emma lifted her head, glaring at him even as she let out one of her old, irrepressible laughs.

'Please tell me you are not actually thinking there was something going on between me and Antonio?' she demanded. 'Because that would, frankly, be completely paranoid and weird, not to mention totally absurd.'

Even though he was still feeling icy inside, Nico managed a laugh. 'Point taken.'

Emma shook her head slowly. 'Why don't you trust me, Nico?'

He shifted in his seat, feeling skewered by her soft, wounded gaze. 'I told you, this is as much about me as it is about you.'

'Is it?' She sighed, clearly not convinced. 'Well, as it happens, I haven't been sure I can trust you. Because of what your cousin said to me at your memorial service.'

'What Antonio said?' He sat up straight, frowning as he searched her resolute yet resigned expression. 'Something more than you've already told me, you mean?'

She took a deep breath, let it out slowly. 'He said he didn't want me sticking around because you'd told him that you'd been tiring of me already. That you'd looked into an annulment or divorce before you'd headed to the Maldives, and if I knew what was good for me,

I'd take the money he offered me gratefully and never come sniffing round him or any of the other Santinis again, because I certainly wouldn't get anything more out of any of you.'

'He said...' Nico's mind was spinning. 'He said I was tiring of you?'

'Yes.' She tilted her chin at that stubbornly determined angle. 'And frankly there was no real reason for me not to believe it. We'd only been married a week, you worked for much of that time, and kept me stuck in your flat without introducing me to anyone, or even telling people you were married, as far as I could see.'

Nico blinked, because he certainly hadn't looked at it that way before. 'It was early days—'

'Sometimes I wondered if you were ashamed of me,' she confessed quietly. 'To be honest, I wouldn't blame you if you were. I was never going to fit into your crowd. But you asked me to marry you so suddenly... I wondered if you'd had cause to regret such an impulsive decision.'

'I had not been looking into either an annulment or divorce,' he stated flatly. He might not remember everything, but he was sure of that.

'But did you regret it?' she challenged. 'Honestly, I wouldn't blame you if you had.'

Expelling a shaky breath, Nico passed a hand over his eyes. He felt pain throb at his temples, like a jungle beat, promising the arrival of a migraine. He strove to keep it at bay. 'I don't know exactly what I thought before I left for the Maldives,' he admitted. 'I can't remember.'

'So you might have been considering a divorce—'

'No, I'm sure of that.' He spoke firmly, while Emma just looked at him, shaking her head slowly.

'Nico, how could you possibly be sure, if you can't remember?'

'Because…because when I woke up from the coma, you were the first face I saw in my mind's eye. The first person I remembered.' He looked away, embarrassed by the admission. He'd never meant to tell her that, to admit to such weakness—that he'd been fixated on a fairy tale while she'd viewed the whole world—and him—with clear-eyed pragmatism.

Emma was silent for a long moment, and he turned back to her, waiting for her response. 'I'm not sure that makes much difference,' she said at last, her voice small and sad. 'What you thought you remembered isn't the same as what really happened.'

'But if we don't know what really happened—'

'Nico, I meant what I said before,' she cut across him quietly, 'that we barely know each other. We only had a month together before the plane crash, and it was a month out of time, out of reality. You don't really know me, know my past, where I've been, what I've done, or even what I'm capable of, and I don't really know any of that about you. With that in mind, I can understand why you didn't trust me, why you would want a paternity test…but can't you understand why I find it hard to trust you?'

Nico stared at her for a long moment, her heartfelt words thudding through him. His head was really starting to ache now, as it often had since the accident, that strange, tickling sensation at the back of his brain worse than ever. Even as he acknowledged the truth of her sentiments, he had a niggling feeling that this would all make more sense if he could just remember…

Remember what?

'Nico?' Emma prompted softly.

'Yes, of course,' he allowed, forcing his mind back to what she'd said, even as his head continued to ache and throb. 'All things considered, I understand what you mean. Our marriage was, it's true, a bit…rushed and abrupt, and we might have both had regrets, but that doesn't change the reality now.'

A small smile played with her mouth, although her eyes were still filled with worry and sorrow. 'Why *did* you marry me, so suddenly, as it happens? I might not know you very well, but it still seems out of character, and you'd made it clear at the beginning that we were only having an affair.'

Yes, he'd set those parameters as he always did, to guard his heart. Too bad it hadn't worked. 'Well.' He cleared his throat. 'I suppose it *was* something of an impulse decision.'

'Yes, clearly, but why?'

Why not be honest about this, as he had been before? Clearly there had been too many secrets in their short-lived relationship, and truth was needed for trust. 'I asked you right after I found out that I wasn't my father's son,' he confessed. 'It was a shock, even though in retrospect it shouldn't have been. And I suppose I wanted to feel…connected…with someone. To be part of a family again, in some way.'

Her eyes widened and her mouth parted softly in surprise. Nico looked away. Why had he said so much?

It made him sound completely pathetic, as if he'd been begging for affection wherever he could find it.

'That phone call...before you came out on the balcony, when you asked me...that was your father? Telling you—'

'Yes, he was giving me the results of the paternity test.' His chest felt tight, and his head was aching abominably now, a thundering in his temples he longed to assuage. He needed to lie down in a dark room, preferably with a cold cloth over his eyes, but first he needed to finish this conversation. He knew how important it was. 'He said it wasn't a surprise, that he'd always been sure, deep down, that I wasn't his, and it didn't change anything for him—meaning, unfortunately, that he had no interest in having a relationship with me.'

'And that was why...' she whispered, shaking her head.

'The next day, before we married, I went to see him. I told him I'd resign, and that was when he refused. We were married that afternoon.' Put like that, it sounded strangely stark, and Emma seemed to think so too, judging by her bleak expression.

She let out a soft laugh, but the sound only held sadness as she looked down at her lap. 'None of it was about me at all, was it?' she surmised quietly. 'I shouldn't be surprised, of course, and I'm not, not really, but...you were right, Nico, when you said this was about you more than it was about me. I just didn't realise quite how much.'

And even though he'd meant that as a reassurance, he saw it wasn't now. She only looked hurt, that his marriage proposal hadn't been because she'd bowled him over, but because he'd been lashing out in his pain. And yet she had affected him more than any other woman...

'Emma...' He pressed his hands to his temples, trying to relieve the pressure that was building there. His stomach churned and his vision was starting to tunnel.

'It's okay, Nico. At least now we know where we were, as well as where we are now. Or,' she corrected with a crooked smile, 'you will when you get the results of the paternity test tomorrow.'

Nico swore softly as he dropped his hands from his head. 'I don't need the results. Not any more.'

'Don't you?'

Yes, damn it, he did, but for *his* sake. Couldn't she see that? Why did it feel as if he was damned one way, condemned another? There was no winning.

'This can be a fresh start,' he insisted, gritting his teeth against the pain in his head. 'For both of us.'

'A fresh start?' She laughed again, once more without humour, but at least it had more life in it, more spirit. 'And what will that look like, exactly?'

'We can decide together.' That was important to him. 'But as to how it will look...' Hell if he knew, he realised. They were still virtual strangers. How were they supposed to figure this out? And his *head*...

He sat back, letting out a breath as his temples continued to throb. He'd been hoping to stave off the migraine, but it was galloping towards him now, pulling him under. He had a few minutes, maybe only a few seconds, before it engulfed him completely. 'We'll figure it out,' he managed, 'and I promise you, I will al-

ways promise you, I will provide for you. I will keep
you safe—' He stopped as the pain took over and he
felt himself sagging forward onto the floor. He tried
to hold himself upright, but the pain was too much,
his vision going black, and the last thing he heard was
Emma's startled cry.

CHAPTER NINE

'NICO.'

Emma dropped to her knees in front of Nico's prone body as his eyelids fluttered closed. Why hadn't she realised he was in pain? She could see it now, in the greyness of his skin, the beads of sweat on his forehead, the way he was clenching his jaw. She'd been reeling from everything he'd told her, all the implications tumbling through her mind, and so she hadn't seen what was right in front of her face. There was a lesson in that, surely, but right now she didn't have time to ponder it.

'Are you hurt?' she demanded, smoothing his hair back from his damp forehead. He forced his eyes open to gaze at her blearily. 'Can you tell me what's wrong?'

'Migraine,' he forced out through pale lips. He grimaced as his eyes closed again. 'I'm sorry, but I think... I think I might be sick.'

Emma scrambled up and ran to the kitchen that was along one wall of the open space. Flinging open cupboards, she found a bowl and brought it back just in time for Nico to retch helplessly into it.

'This is bonding, isn't it?' she told him on a shaky

laugh, determined to see the bright side of things. 'First, I was the one who was sick, and now you are. I suppose it will be my turn again next. Where's your handkerchief when you need it?'

'In…my right-hand pocket,' he managed in a croaky whisper.

She laughed again, softly, and reached for the small square of cotton, dabbing his lips with it. He smiled faintly and her heart twisted, a sharp pain beneath her breastbone.

Don't start now, Emma, she cautioned herself. *Don't start falling for him again, just because he smiles at you.*

After the emotional whirlwind of the last twenty-four hours, that was the last thing she needed. She had to keep a cool head. Her heart, too.

'Are you going to be sick again?' she asked gently, and he shook his head.

'I don't think so…thankfully.'

'Do you have any painkillers or medication?'

He nodded and then managed, 'It's in my washbag, in the bathroom. A brown bottle.'

'I'll get it.'

She found it easily enough, noting the prescription was to be taken as needed, in the case of migraines. Back in the living room, Nico had tried to ease himself into a sitting position, only to slump back down again, with a grimace. He had to hate being seen as so weak, Emma realised with a wry pang. She might not know a lot about him, but she knew he was a proud man, and he'd admitted a lot to her today. A lot of weakness and vulnerability. She realised it made him more appealing to her, not less, as he might have thought. As to their future…well, she couldn't think about that just yet.

'Let me help you to bed.'

'I can do it—'

'No,' she replied with a laugh and a shake of her head, 'you really can't. Not unless you want to crawl there on your hands and knees. Let me help you, Nico.'

With no real choice but to acquiesce, he nodded, and she was able to help him to his feet as he struggled to manage as much as he could on his own, even though his face was taut with pain, his whole body tense. Somehow, with one arm around his shoulders and another around his waist, Emma managed to help him stumble to bed. He collapsed on top of the sheets with a groan as she took off his shoes, unbuttoned his shirt and trousers while he gazed up at her through half-closed lids.

'Are you ravishing me, Signora Santini?' he asked, his voice slightly slurred from the pain, as well as, no doubt, the heavy medication he'd been given that was now kicking in.

She laughed as she slid his trousers from his legs, admittedly enjoying the feeling of his powerful thighs and taut calves under her hands. He had a beautiful, powerful body, even if he seemed weak as a kitten now. 'I'd certainly have to be the one to ravish you rather than the other way round, considering the state of you right now,' she teased as she dropped his trousers onto the floor.

He gazed up at her through half-closed lids, wearing only his boxers and unbuttoned shirt, his tautly muscled chest visible through the parted fabric. He looked as sexy as a male centrefold, Emma acknowledged, even with his grey, pain-filled face.

'You could let me try, at least...' he mumbled, reaching one hand up to her before it fell slackly to his side.

'Some try, Casanova.' Emma brushed a lock of hair from his forehead, disarmed by his obvious vulnerability and even more dismayed by her own reaction to it—a sudden, surprising welling up of tenderness. It had been better, she realised, when he'd been arrogant and angry, because it had been much easier to keep her distance. Or even when she'd worried she couldn't trust him—because she knew she did now. She trusted him and she *liked* him, and she knew she really couldn't afford to feel that way. Not now, and not ever. Letting someone in was too risky. She knew that, and so, it seemed, did Nico. They'd both, in their own ways, been hurt by their families, by the love they'd offered but hadn't had accepted. She didn't think either of them wanted to risk in the same way again. If they were going to stay married, it was going to have to be one strictly of convenience, no tender emotions involved.

Which was a much-needed reminder in this particular moment.

'You should sleep,' she said as she pulled the duvet up over him and, with his eyes fluttering closed once more, he reached out to her, encircling her wrist with his fingers, the touch enough to cause a shower of sparks racing all the way up her arm, a swift blaze of yearning to start in her centre. Maybe she would ravish him after all...

'Stay with me?' he asked, his voice low and rough, and her desire melted into something deeper. Something dangerous that she kept trying to steel herself against.

'But you need to sleep...'

'Please?'

It was the please that did it, the unabashed yearning in his voice. 'Yes, all right,' she said, and he pulled her towards him until she fitted against him, her head on his shoulder, the steady thud of his heart beneath her cheek, her body curled into his. They'd lain like this during their one month together, she remembered, and every time it had been bittersweet.

Bitter, because she'd tried to caution herself against feeling too much, trusting too much, and sweet because he'd made her feel safe and wanted and even loved. There hadn't been love involved, not really, she *knew* that, and, more importantly, there wouldn't be this time, either.

But could they forge some kind of future together, for the sake of their child? Could they learn to get along, to like one another, to be a family? Could she trust him with her child, if not her heart?

Maybe she could, she thought sleepily, her eyes fluttering closed as she snuggled closer to Nico. Maybe, if they both kept their heads—and definitely their hearts—this could work out. It could work out wonderfully.

Nico lowered his phone as he stared out at the hazy blue sky, the city shimmering under the late morning sunlight.

'Your wife is really rather unwell, Signor Santini. Something simply must be done.'

The OB's words, spoken so censoriously, still rang in his ears. She hadn't added *and that's your fault*, but she might as well have done. He certainly felt it was.

What had he been thinking, dragging Emma around the city, forcing pointless confrontations, when she was pregnant, tired and emotionally overwrought? And, as the OB had told him, underweight, seriously anaemic, and with high blood pressure. He'd thought she'd looked a little pale and gaunt when he'd first seen her, but he'd had no idea of the seriousness of the situation. And now he needed to rectify it. Immediately.

He took a deep breath and squared his shoulders, doing his best to banish the remnants of yesterday's headache that still lingered at his temples. He'd slept for sixteen hours straight, right around the clock, waking this morning to an empty bed and the phone ringing—the OB telling him what she'd learned about Emma, all of it alarming and even disturbing. He'd had no idea about so much…and, he realised, he still didn't, at least not entirely. Not enough. But he wanted to.

He ran a hand through his shower-damp hair and turned to the bedroom door, needing to find Emma.

'You're finally up,' she said from her seat at the breakfast bar. She'd been flicking through one of the designer magazines the hotel provided but she pushed it aside now; smiling tentatively as he came into the room. For a second, a memory of sleepy warmth, her body snugly next to his, had lingered in his mind like the vestiges of a dream. Had she slept in the bed with him, cuddled up together? She might have, but he couldn't really remember; the medication had knocked him out.

Right now what he could remember, all too clearly, was how she'd seen him—weak, sick, *being* sick, stumbling to bed. Hardly his best self, and yet somehow she was still smiling as she looked at him, and things between them felt easier. Less tense, even though the OB's warning words still weighed heavily in his gut.

'I'm sorry I slept so long,' he said as he went to the kitchen area to pour himself some coffee. Emma twisted around in her seat to track him with her gaze.

'I'm glad you did,' she said. 'You needed it, clearly.'

'You need your sleep, too.' He turned to face her, leaning against the counter as he cradled his coffee cup. She looked fresh-faced and artless this morning, her hair piled on top of her head in a messy bun, wearing a long, loose sundress with a button-down shirt open over it, yet he still saw how pale she seemed, and how thin, her wrists poking out from the cuffs of her shirt. 'The OB called me just now,' he told her.

'She did?' Emma's sunny, open expression immediately turned guarded, alert, in a way that made him feel both guilty and sad. 'Why did she call you, and not me?'

'Because she wanted to yell at me, I think.' He smiled wryly and her expression lightened, just a little, which made him glad. 'She's emailing you the results of all the tests, as she said she would yesterday.'

'There's only one test that really matters though, isn't there?' She didn't speak with any rancour or bitterness, but Nico felt it all the same. No matter how he'd explained how demanding the paternity test really had been about him, he knew it had hurt her, just as he knew he was sorry for that. Sorrier than he'd expected to be, considering what he'd just learned.

'That test was conclusive,' he replied quietly. 'I am the baby's father, as you told me, and as I really knew all along.' He might have jumped to conclusions because it had felt easier, or at least stronger, to be angry rather than hurt, but the reality was, he knew, that he'd never truly doubted Emma. 'I'm sorry for questioning you,' he told her.

She let out one of her irrepressible laughs, her mouth twitching. 'An apology! I'm so honoured.'

He frowned, because she made it sound as if he never said sorry, and he did, surely... 'I apologise when I'm in the wrong,' he told her, although it came out just a little bit like a question.

'Which obviously isn't very often, then,' Emma returned tartly, even though she was still smiling. 'I think that's the first one I've heard.'

'Is it?' He blinked at her, surprised, and she laughed again.

'Perhaps this is the time for a bit of self-awareness, then,' she teased. 'You do have the habit of being a bit...autocratic. Dare I say it...arrogant?' She bit her lip, widening her eyes, and while he knew she was just teasing—sort of—there was more than a sting of truth in her words.

He really had been riding a wave of self-righteous fury, Nico acknowledged, ever since he'd walked into her wedding—or maybe, he realised with a jolt, even before that. When he'd taken her away from that restaurant, swept her up into his own privileged world, he'd felt like her rescuer. He'd liked showering her with attention and gifts, having her look up to him, dependent on him, even a little bit in awe. He certainly hadn't treated her like an equal partner in their short-lived marriage—as Emma had pointed out, he hadn't introduced her to anyone, hadn't tried to really include her in his life. Hadn't even thought of it.

The knowledge was uncomfortable, shaming. Maybe it was a result of a childhood of never feeling as if he could do or be enough to his father, but he'd definitely enjoyed being Emma's everything, for a little while. Making himself the centre of her world, because he'd never been that before. But was that how any relationship, never mind a marriage, was really supposed to be?

'Nico?' she prompted. 'You are frowning pretty ferociously. You know I was kidding, right? Well.' Her smile widened. 'Sort of, anyway.'

'Right.' He was frowning, Nico knew, because having these realisations about himself really wasn't comfortable, even if it was necessary. 'Well, then, I'm sorry I haven't been willing to admit when I'm wrong,' he told her. 'There—that's two sorrys in the space of a few minutes, so consider yourself doubly honoured.'

She grinned at him, eyes dancing. 'Must be a record.'

'Must be.' He took a sip of his coffee, trying to order his thoughts for the conversation he knew they needed to have. He'd marched in here, about to tell Emma his plans—that he was taking her away, taking care of her as she so clearly needed, and all without her having so much as a say in it. Suddenly that didn't seem like such a good idea.

'The OB mentioned a few other things,' he told her at last, choosing his words with care. 'She'll tell the same to you, but she told me because she felt I should do something about it.'

'I did tell her she could share my medical records with you,' Emma replied with a defiant shrug, although her expression had turned wary. 'I had nothing to hide.'

'I know.' Nothing to hide, but there were still things she hadn't told him. Hadn't wanted to tell him, perhaps, because like him she didn't like sharing what seemed to be weaknesses. Admitting vulnerability.

'So, do something about what?' Emma straightened in her chair, her gaze serious.

'Your health.' He came to sit next to her at the table, regarding her sombrely. 'You're worryingly underweight, apparently, as well as anaemic. And the OB believes you've been stressed, which isn't good for the baby, obviously.' And there were other things she'd told him too, things from her childhood that made him ache. Made him want to protect Emma with everything he had. Everything he was.

'Oh. Wow.' Emma folded her arms, hunching her shoulders. 'Well, I knew I was a little bit underweight from when I went to the clinic a couple of weeks ago, because of the morning sickness, but that is getting better, now that I'm starting the second trimester.' She sounded defensive, a little hurt, and that made him ache all the more.

'The OB wasn't blaming you, Emma, and I'm not,

either.' He realised that was where she was going with this, and it was not the takeaway he intended at all. 'If anything, I'm blaming myself. I marched in here and dragged you around and didn't think about your condition—'

'You didn't know about my condition at first, and, in any case, it's only been a couple of days. I was underweight and I guess anaemic before you came on the scene, Nico, so you don't need to blame yourself.' She rallied, cocking her head as she gave him a teasing smile even though she still looked worried. 'That's the other side of arrogance—you think everything is your fault.' She tapped his chest playfully. 'The world does not revolve around you, you know.'

'I know.' But he'd wanted it to, he realised. Was that why he'd been so determined to be with Emma, to marry her? Because after his parents' revelations, he'd wanted to be the centre of someone's world, and he'd known from the start that she was alone and vulnerable. It hardly put him in an admirable light, but at least he was aware of it now. He could choose to be different; he could choose for their relationship to be different. Instead of being the centre of Emma's world, she could be the centre of his. Emma and their child. Nothing else, he knew, was as important as they were.

'The main thing now,' he told her, 'is to get you healthy again. Give you time to rest, relax, eat good food and grow our baby.' And recover in ways he hadn't realised she'd needed to.

Her pupils flared and a small smile touched her mouth. 'You sound rather protective all of a sudden.'

'I feel protective.' She had no idea of just how much.

'All right, then.' She shrugged. 'I promise I'll eat better. Where's my prenatal vitamin?'

She was teasing, but he was utterly serious. 'They're being delivered this morning, along with some iron pills for the anaemia. But I was thinking of taking a few more proactive steps, Emma.'

She raised her eyebrows, looking uncertain and trying to hide it with her usual spirited insouciance. 'Such as?'

He hesitated, and then admitted, 'I have a villa on a private island in the Mediterranean. It's a very peaceful place, completely secluded. I thought we could go there for a few weeks. You could rest and recover, and so could I, for that matter. As you saw yesterday, I'm not completely over the effects of the accident.'

'How is your head?' she asked, reaching one hand out as if to touch him but then dropping it before she did. He wished she hadn't; he welcomed her touch.

'It's a lot better than it was yesterday,.but I think we could both use a bit of a break. And…it could be a chance to get to know one another properly. Because even though we're married, you were right when you said we barely knew each other. That month we had together was a bit surreal, wasn't it?' He smiled crookedly. Surreal, yes, but also wonderful, in its own way. Now, however, was the time for reality…however that looked. However it felt.

She smiled uncertainly, her gaze scanning his face, as if looking for clues. 'Okay, so we stay on your island for a few weeks. Then what?'

Then what, indeed. 'That's up for discussion,' Nico answered slowly, although he knew now what he wanted. 'We're married, and we're going to be a family. How that looks is up to both of us.'

'Wow, have you been taking a class or something?' Emma teased, and Nico shook his head, smiling.

'No, but you've been schooling me, I guess.'

'Ha.' She shook her head back at him as they smiled at each other, and it felt both silly and rather wonderful. Nico eased back, determined to stay logical. Pragmatic. He wanted to do this right, and that meant not engaging his emotions too much.

'Well.' Emma looked down at the floor, a tendril of wavy golden-brown hair falling in front of her face, obscuring her expression from his view. 'I suppose I don't really know the answer to that.' She glanced up, peeping at him from behind her hair. 'What do *you* want it to look like?'

Nico sat back, considering the question. 'Santini Enterprises is based in Rome, so I'll need to be there for work on occasion, but once the baby comes, I suppose we'd want more space than a flat in the city.'

'Even though that flat is palatial,' she teased.

'Maybe you want to be involved in choosing our home,' Nico suggested. 'We could buy somewhere new, something you've picked yourself.' He liked the idea. A fresh start, away from his family, the memories, everything. A fresh start for the two of them, whatever that ended up looking like.

'I could pick?' She sounded so incredulous that Nico glanced at her, frowning.

'Well, we'd pick together, I suppose, but why not?'

She shook her head slowly. 'It's just… I've never…'

She let out a rather wobbly laugh. 'I've never had my own home before.'

'You haven't?' His frown deepened as he realised again how little he actually knew about her, although he was starting to understand, or at least to guess, with the glimmers of knowledge both the doctor and Emma herself had given him about the lack in her childhood—lack of love and, it seemed, lack of even basic care. Evidence of cruelty too, which infuriated and saddened him in equal measure. But, he reminded himself, things could be different now. For Emma, for him, for them. And a few weeks on a private island together would give them abundant opportunity to get to know each other—in every way possible.

CHAPTER TEN

ONCE AGAIN, just as she had when she'd first met—
and married—Nico Santini, Emma felt the need to
pinch herself. To scrunch her eyes shut and then open
them wide again, to make sure this wasn't all a glori-
ous dream that was going to evaporate as soon as she
looked at it too closely.

'Make yourself comfortable,' Nico said as he
strolled into the main cabin area of the Santini private jet. He'd told her he usually travelled business
class for environmental reasons, but he'd used Santini Enterprises' private plane to get to Los Angeles
as quickly as possible, and now they needed to take it
back again, to Rome. To her new life.

A shiver of both excitement and apprehension rip-
pled through her at the thought. Everything had moved
so quickly, it was hard to believe it was only forty-eight
hours since Nico had interrupted her wedding, twenty-
four since he had done something of an about-turn,
becoming consideration itself, kindness personified...
just as he'd been when they'd first met.

Back then she'd told herself to be cautious, even
as she'd ridden the wave of luxury and pleasure, let

herself enjoy it all because it had been so utterly different from the rest of her life, and she'd been sure it would end eventually...which it had. Second time round she fully intended to be more cautious, more careful. Things could change on a dime, and yet...

It was hard not to buy into the fantasy, the fairy tale, at least a little. Hard not to want something she'd never had, and yet she knew she needed to keep herself from it, if she could. Stay smart and safe, because while Nico seemed intent on building a new life together, Emma intended to remain guarded, at least a little. Guard her heart, if she could, because she knew how much it hurt when you tried to love someone and they let you down. Time and time again, from her mother when she was a baby to the foster mum who turned away to the man, years ago, when she'd been reeling from leaving care—they'd all walked away without a backward glance while you were left gasping and shattered.

'Emma? No, absolutely not. Sorry...that was never going to be a possibility.'

Her foster mother's words, and her firm and certain tone, still haunted her in her weaker moments, when she remembered how much she'd hoped, *believed*... And for nothing. Always for nothing.

It had been the same with Eric, the man she'd convinced herself she loved simply because she'd wanted to *be* loved. A brief fling, and he'd left her without a thought. She'd tried to act as if she hadn't cared, hoping that maybe then she wouldn't.

All those painful experiences had taught her a hard yet necessary lesson, and she knew now that she most definitely wasn't ever going to open herself up to that kind of pain again. Since Nico didn't seem to want to either, she hoped they really could make this work. Or so she kept telling herself.

'This plane is amazing,' she remarked, running her hand over the buttery leather of a built-in sofa on one side of the main cabin, facing another sofa, a low coffee table between them, with a bowl of exotic-looking fruit its centrepiece.

'I'll give you the full tour before we take off.' He smiled at her, and she tried to ignore the fizzing sensation in her stomach the mere curve of his lips caused. *That* was an aspect of their marriage she was both looking forward to and feeling extremely apprehensive about, because she knew when Nico touched her she forgot everything, especially how to guard her heart, and she needed to stay careful. Controlled. As soon as he touched her, all her resolutions could be blown to smithereens, and where would that leave her?

Nowhere she wanted to be.

'Sure,' she told him, smiling back, trying to ignore that fizzing, the way his jade gaze lingered on her, making her body heat, her blood surge, and her mind remember how it had been between them before. 'That would be great.'

'Come on, then.' He kept one hand on the small of her back—his palm searing her through the thin material of her T-shirt—as he guided her to the back of the plane. 'This is the study,' he said, opening a door to a room with a large desk and a couple of leather club chairs, a wall lined with bookshelves.

'I feel like I'm on Air Force One,' she told him, not

altogether joking. The private plane was really like nothing she'd ever seen before, nothing she could even imagine. She'd had a month of living in Nico's luxurious world, but it had never felt as real and permanent as it did now, on their way to his private island. A whole island, to himself. Even after the luxury hotels and flats from before, this was definitely next level.

'It's convenient for work,' he replied with a shrug.

'Do you know, I don't even know what you really do for Santini Enterprises.' She turned from her perusal of the shelves, mostly books on economics and business, with a few classics of literature thrown in. 'You said your father said you were the face of the operation, but what does that mean, exactly?'

Nico propped one powerful shoulder against the doorframe as he folded his arms. 'I handle all the deals, basically,' he told her. 'Santini Enterprises has a lot of different interests—resorts, like the one in the Maldives I was going to see, as well as hotels, tech companies, a few other things. My father loves to acquire businesses, sell the ones he doesn't need, and buy more. I manage the negotiations.'

'Do you enjoy it?'

He looked startled, as if the question had never occurred to him. 'I don't know if I do or not,' he replied slowly. 'I like closing a deal, I suppose, but I never really thought about doing anything else. Working for Santini Enterprises was always going to be in my future. I was never given the choice to consider any other options.' He grimaced slightly. 'Even though my father resented the fact that he suspected I wasn't his son, he still wanted me to take over the family business. Sometimes I've wondered why, if it was just a point of pride.'

'Pride can be a very powerful thing.' After all, Nico was a proud man. Had it been pride that had taken him all the way to California in search of her, or something more? Emma wasn't sure, and she wasn't brave enough to ask. 'And if you had been,' she asked instead, 'what would you do? Your dream job. What would that be?'

He let out a little laugh, the sound one of uncertainty that made Emma's heart both ache and melt in a way she wasn't entirely comfortable with but couldn't keep herself from. As wealthy and privileged as he'd been his whole life, she realised, Nico's experiences oddly mirrored her own. A lack of choice. A fear, even an inability, perhaps, to let yourself dream. She hadn't expected such a point of similarity.

'I suppose,' he answered slowly, his arms folded as he leaned his head back against the door, 'I'd like to do something similar, but on my own, and for smaller companies that don't usually get a look-in. A venture capitalist, of a sort, but for grass-roots operations, home-grown businesses who need the opportunity.'

She smiled, envisaging the kind of businesses he meant—companies that started in someone's garage, a stay-at-home mum turning her kitchen into a bakery, a high-school geek making his tech ideas into millions. 'I like the sound of that.'

'Do you?'

He lifted his head so his jade-green gaze blazed into hers, both searching and finding, and her breath caught in her chest as her heart started to race. A moment of friendly solidarity morphed, in an instant, into something else. Something more.

'I like the idea of looking after the little guys,' she replied a bit unsteadily, 'since I've always been one.'

'Is that how you've felt? Like a little guy?'

She shrugged. 'If a little guy is someone who never has the power or opportunity or choice? Yes. Pretty much. But I haven't always been great about making opportunities for myself. That can be scary, on your own, which is why I think it would be great if you helped people like that along. Partnered with them.' She hadn't meant to reveal quite so much, and so she continued, a bit hurriedly, 'I think you'd be good at that, too, actually. Giving people the courage as well as the opportunity to raise the bar...' She trailed off because her mind was hopelessly buzzing and he was looking at her with such heat, such blatant need. When had anyone, anyone other than Nico, looked at her like that? Made her feel like this—important and, most of all, wanted? Very wanted.

'Emma...' He took a step towards her and she held her breath, waiting for his touch. Craving it, because she knew how it made her feel. How his hand skimming along her skin could create sparks, a raging fire. And how that fire could consume her, burn away all her good intentions to guard her heart...

But she couldn't think about any of that now. She could only think about him, coming closer, about to touch her, consume her. They hadn't touched since that sleepy fumble in bed that had awakened her body, made her remember all too well how he felt. How he made her feel—and wanted to feel again.

Last night, exhausted by everything, she'd gone to bed early while Nico had stayed up making preparations for their trip, and Emma had wondered when— not if, not any more—they would come together again. They would make this marriage real for a second time, even better than before.

He took another step towards her, reaching for her hand, lacing his fingers through hers as he tugged her gently towards him. 'I'm glad you're here,' he said softly, and she gave a little, unsteady laugh.

'So am I.' Although she was still afraid. Afraid of falling for this man who was doing everything right— something she knew not to trust.

'We can make this work,' Nico murmured as he drew her ever closer, so her hips bumped his and heat flared deep inside, along with an almost unbearable yearning. 'Can't we?'

'I'd...like to think so.' Although she was having trouble thinking right now, with Nico's body so close to hers, the scent of his cologne—of him—in her nostrils, making her dizzy. His fingers skimmed her cheek, tucking a tendril of hair behind her ear, and leaving a fiery trail of longing in its wake. Emma's lips parted soundlessly. Nico dipped his head. Her heart tripped, caught, tripped again. He was going to kiss her...

'Signor Santini?' The flight attendant's discreet cough had Nico dropping his hand and Emma springing away, her heart now juddering. 'We're ready to take off.'

'Thank you, Enrico.' Nico's voice was calm although Emma saw the spots of colour high on his cheekbones. He had been as affected as she was by their almost-kiss, and the realisation was wonderfully thrilling. She, who had never had anyone care about her enough to be affected by anything she did, could make this man's breathing ragged and his face heat with desire.

But you can't make him love you, so don't even try.

The reminder was painful but necessary. As long as she kept everything in perspective, Emma told herself, she'd be okay. She'd be safe—from the dangerous treacheries of her own heart.

'Pity I didn't get to show you the bedroom,' Nico murmured as he stepped closer to her, his breath tickling her ear. 'But I will later.'

Was that a promise? Before she could reply, he continued, his voice low, 'That part of our relationship is not in doubt, Emma, but we'll resume it only when you're ready to. You can be assured of that. I have no interest in pressuring you in that way.'

More consideration and kindness. Tears stung her eyes, even as her body still tingled. She was on emotional overload, and it was dangerous. Frightening. Emma drew a steadying breath.

'Thank you,' she said, and he let his fingers skim her cheek one last time, so she struggled not to close her eyes, lean into the caress.

'Although I must admit I hope it's sooner rather than later,' he told her, his voice a wry rumble. 'Because you're just about killing me here.'

She let out another unsteady laugh and then followed him out of the study to the main cabin, where they took their seats.

* * *

Nico gazed out of the window of the plane at the stretch of azure sky and felt a glow of satisfaction deep inside—as well as a very much *unsatisfied* ache of longing. That would be dealt with in time, he was sure, and very pleasurably so. He had no doubts about that. He just needed to wait for Emma to feel as ready as he was.

He had come to realise a few things about his wife over the last few days, as well as remembering their month together from before. Things that, taken individually, hadn't struck him overmuch, but now which were starting to come together to form a whole, surprising picture.

Yesterday the OB had told him that Emma had not had many of her childhood vaccinations, and her check-up had revealed a few worrying details—a wrist broken as a small child that hadn't been set properly and so had healed at a slightly awkward angle, something he noticed now as she sat across from him, one elbow propped on the arm rest, her gaze distant and thoughtful. There was a bump where her wrist met her hand, small and virtually unnoticeable, unless you were looking for it, which he was.

'I'm telling you these things, first of all, because Emma herself gave me permission to share her medical details with you,' the OB had said. 'Otherwise, of course, I would not be saying a single word. But also because she has clearly not had proper medical care for long stretches of time in her life, and I want to make sure she gets that care now.'

'She will, absolutely,' Nico had replied, his voice

gruff, his mind reeling from other things the OB had said—that Emma had shown signs of childhood malnourishment; that there were scars on her leg that could be cigarette burns.

'She didn't use the word abuse,' the OB had said, 'when she was talking to me, but clearly there were elements of it in her childhood. I trust she will be safe with you.'

'On my life,' Nico had promised. 'On my *life*.'

Now he turned from his view of the sky to Emma, curled up across from him. 'It's eleven hours from here to Rome,' he said, 'so this might be as good a time as any to get to know one another.'

The look Emma gave as she turned to him was definitely wary. Just like him, she didn't enjoy talking about her childhood, herself, and he was starting to understand why Nico relaxed back into his seat. 'But first let me get you something to drink, eat.'

A small smile quirked her mouth. 'You're always feeding me, it seems.'

'I like feeding you, and you need fattening up.' He pressed a discreet button in the armrest of his seat and Enrico came swiftly into the main cabin.

'Signor Santini?'

Nico glanced at Emma. 'What would you like?'

She shrugged, laughing. 'I don't even know. Umm…some crackers?'

'That's it?' Nico couldn't keep from sounding disapproving, and she rolled her eyes.

'And some cheese.'

'What kind?'

'What kind do you have?'

'This plane is well stocked, Emma. We pretty much have whatever you want.'

She laughed softly. 'It's going to take me a while to get used to this. Okay, I'll have some Cheddar then, please.' She glanced at Enrico. 'Thank you.'

'My pleasure, Signora Santini.'

He left the room while Emma shook her head slowly. 'Signora Santini. I'm going to have to get used to that.'

'You were Signora Santini before,' Nico pointed out.

'Yes, but no one ever really called me that. I barely saw anyone in the week we were married.'

Nico frowned. 'I don't think I quite realised that at the time. I don't entirely remember...'

'It's okay, Nico.' She leaned over to brush the back of his hand with the tips of her fingers. 'It wasn't just about you. It was me, too. I know we were married, we *are* married, but I think part of me was always bracing myself for you to change your mind...which was why I believed Antonio when he said I was already on the way out.'

A blaze of anger fired through him. He would definitely need to have words with his cousin. 'But why were you? Bracing yourself, I mean?'

She shrugged. 'Because it happened so fast. Because you're rich and powerful and attractive as all get-out, and I'm...' she trailed off with a shrug before finishing with one of her old laughs '...not.'

'Rich and powerful, perhaps not, but attractive as— what did you say? All get-out?'

A playful smile quirked her mouth. 'Mm-hmm.'

'You are definitely that.' He leaned over to tuck a

tendril of hair behind her ear, letting his fingers linger on her cheek, her skin soft and cool beneath his touch. Her eyes fluttered closed briefly and Nico ran his thumb along her lips as a shudder escaped her.

'Nico...'

'I can't keep from touching you,' he admitted as he traced the outline of her lips. 'Do you mind?'

'Mind?' She let out an unsteady laugh, her breath hitching. 'No.'

'Good.' He leaned forward, just as the door to the cabin opened.

'Signora Santini? Your cheese and crackers.'

Nico smiled wryly even as his heart thudded in response to that simple touch. 'It seems we are always being interrupted,' he told Emma sotto voce, and she smiled back, her face flushed, her breathing still unsteady.

'Thank you, Enrico,' she said, and the attendant withdrew again, leaving them alone.

'So,' Nico said, determined not to be distracted again—although what a lovely distraction it was—'we were going to get to know one another.'

'Is that what you were doing?' she teased, eyebrows raised, as she piled Cheddar on top of a cracker and took a large bite.

'I suppose there are different ways of accomplishing that goal,' he agreed wryly. And some were more pleasurable than others. 'But for now, considering the likelihood of us being interrupted yet again, we'll keep it to conversation.'

Her eyes danced as she brushed crumbs from her lips. 'Pity.'

Indeed it was a pity, and he was glad—very glad—she thought so as well. It made his blood sing to think they would remedy that situation one day—or night—soon. Very soon, he hoped. 'Indeed,' he managed, shifting in his seat to ease the persistent ache in his groin. 'But as for now, tell me about yourself. Where did you grow up?'

It seemed an innocuous enough question, but it was as if a veil had dropped down over Emma's face, behind her eyes. Her expression stilled and she put down the rest of her cracker, brushing her hands before tucking them under her thighs. 'Mainly in upstate New York,' she said, her tone as cautious and careful as the expression on her face. 'But I moved around a bit.'

'Yes, I think you mentioned as much before.' But not much else, and he hadn't asked. He hadn't wanted to delve into the past, either hers or his, back then. He'd simply wanted to revel in the moment, to blot out anything else.

Now he felt differently. Now he wanted—needed—to know.

'How come you moved around?'

She shrugged. 'That's just the way it was.'

He leaned forward, lowering his voice, trying to keep his tone gentle. 'You sound as if you don't want to talk about it.'

She sighed and looked out of the window at the blaze of bright blue sky. 'I don't, not particularly, but I suppose you should know at least the basics.' She took a deep breath, squared her shoulders, and then turned back to look at him. 'I was taken away from my mother when I was six months old, due to neglect.

She tried to get me back a year later and failed.' She hesitated and then admitted quietly, 'That was part of my fear, initially, and why I was reluctant to tell you about the baby. Our baby. Because I was scared you might take him or her away from me.'

'Away from you?' Nico sat back, his mouth agape, unable to keep the horror from his face, his voice. 'Emma, I would never do that.'

'I think I know that now,' she admitted a bit shakily, 'but considering what happened to my own mother... I was scared.'

He frowned. 'But your mother neglected you?'

'So they said. I don't actually know. The case files reveal very little. And trust me, when you've gone through the foster system, you see how, despite the best intentions, good people sometimes get taken advantage of and bad people can get a free pass.' She shrugged, and he knew she must have seen that in her own life. The broken wrist, the burns. How much had Emma suffered?

'Whether that happened to my mother or not, I don't know. She died when I was two, a car accident. And I never knew my father—so I suppose we have that in common.' The smile she gave him was wry, determined, and made him ache because it felt so brave. 'I was bounced around from foster family to foster family until I was thirteen, when I was considered too old and frankly too much of a handful for families, and so I ended up in a care home. They're not as bad as you might think,' she added quickly, before he could say anything. 'In some ways, they're better. You can stop trying so hard, to get a family to like you. Want to keep you.'

They had that in common too, he realised. Trying to win people's love. All in all, it sounded like an absolutely wretched childhood. 'And what happened then?' he asked quietly.

'I aged out of the system at eighteen.' She shrugged. 'Again, not as bad as you think. They give you some support, they don't just dump you in it, although by that time it's usually not enough. Most of us feel a little lost. I know I did. But I enrolled in a catering course—I've always liked cooking. I had dreams of opening my own restaurant one day.' She ducked her head a bit, as if this was revealing too much. 'But as it happens, I dropped out after a year.'

'Why?'

'This is starting to feel a bit like an interrogation.' He thought she was trying to sound playful and not quite managing it.

'I don't mean it to be. You can ask me questions too, you know.'

She arched an eyebrow. 'Suddenly you're an open book?'

He shrugged, determined to keep going. Keep trying. 'I'll try to be.'

She let out another breath as she turned to the window. 'I don't even know what to ask.'

'Anything,' he replied, hoping he meant it.

She turned to face him. 'Have you ever been in love?'

Nico tried to keep his expression interested but bland as her question jolted through him. *Had he?* He thought of the affairs he'd had in the past, meaningless flings he'd never even tried to go deeper with, because he hadn't wanted to take that risk, and in any case none of the women had seemed worth it. And as for Emma…well, he'd tried to convince himself he was in love with her, had let that notion carry him through his rehabilitation…but he knew now that you couldn't love someone if you didn't know them. What he'd felt had been infatuation, maybe even obsession, but not love, no matter how much he'd tried to convince himself otherwise. 'No,' he said, and knew he was speaking the truth. 'Have you?'

'No, definitely not.' She spoke decisively. 'All right, another question. Do you want to be in love? Fall in love?'

She clearly wasn't pulling her punches. Nico hesitated, determined to be honest, even if it was risky. 'Considering you're married to me,' he remarked lightly, 'is the question you're really asking, do I want to fall in love with you?'

A startled look passed across Emma's face, like a bird taking flight. 'I suppose,' she finally answered slowly.

And how was he meant to answer that? Nico wondered, realising the trap he'd neatly laid for himself. He'd started out on this venture determined not to fall in love with Emma—the Emma he'd thought he'd known, that he couldn't trust. He'd wanted the kind of arrangement where he reaped all the benefits and yet risked nothing, certainly not his heart. Right now that seemed like a poor exchange, indeed, especially when he was realising Emma wasn't anything like the heartless gold-digger of his imagination. But was he ready to admit to her what—and how much—he did want? He wasn't even sure he could admit it to himself. He wasn't sure he knew...although he thought he might be beginning to suspect.

'I'll answer first,' Emma said, before he could formulate a reply, 'since you seem to be thinking about it. I'm not interested in falling in love, *being* in love, at all. You might as well know I dropped out of that catering course because of a guy. No one important, really, but after I'd aged out of the system I was feeling a little lost, like I said, and I pinned all my hopes on him. Clearly a mistake.' Her mouth twisted. 'But it was more than that, really. The truth was, I was scared of failing. Better to quit than to fail—that, unfortunately, has been my motto for a lot of my life. But in terms of the guy... Eric...' She took a steadying breath, let it out slowly. 'I didn't love him, not really, but I tried to convince myself I did, and unfortunately, he ended up being just like everybody else.'

'Like everybody else?' Nico probed, wondering just what that meant.

'Not interested in sticking around for the long haul.' She hunched her shoulders, tilted her chin, a heartbreaking combination of courage and hurt. 'But even before that, I'd pretty much made my mind up about that sort of thing. I basically grew up on my own, and I've liked it that way. I don't want to...need people like that. Emotionally, I mean. I choose not to, because... well, because it's easier. There was one family who I thought...' She stopped, shaking her head. 'Anyway.

That's how I've lived my life, and that's how I want to keep on living it. Friendship, affection, trust…all good.' She gave him a determined smile. 'But love, no.'

Which he could, unfortunately, understand. Hadn't he been a bit similar—choosing not to try to win his father's love because he realised he could never earn it? But it had been a hard and hopeless way to live, and he wasn't sure he wanted it now, or in the future.

'Don't you have anything to say?' Emma challenged.

'I suppose I understand why you would feel that way,' Nico replied after a moment.

'And that's okay with you?' she pressed. 'I mean, considering your own background, I sort of assumed it would be. That you're not interested in…that kind of thing, either.' She glanced at him, her amber eyes filled with uncertainty, but also, Nico thought, a wary sort of hope. But what was she hoping for? That he agreed with her—or that he didn't?

'Emma,' he said finally, 'we're just getting to know each other now. It all feels a bit precipitous to put limits on our relationship, but certainly, I see your point. We've both been hurt before. It's understandable that we'd both want to take measures to make sure that doesn't happen again.'

She bit her lip, her uncertain gaze scanning his face. Nico kept his expression deliberately bland. 'So it's okay with you?' she pressed again, and he nodded.

'Yes, of course,' he told her, because what else could he say? This was the only thing she wanted to hear, and he didn't know his own heart yet. 'It's okay with me,' he reassured her, and Emma nodded. As she sat back against her seat, Nico couldn't decide if she looked disappointed—or relieved.

CHAPTER ELEVEN

THIS PLACE WAS, Emma thought, far from the first time, utterly amazing. She stood on the terrace off her sumptuous bedroom in Nico's villa as she watched the sun set over the tranquil, aquamarine waters of the Mediterranean Sea lapping the white sand beach at the bottom of the villa's landscaped gardens.

They had arrived at his private island yesterday, after the overnight flight to Rome, where they'd left the Santini private jet and boarded a small hire plane to fly directly to the island, a few miles from Capri, near the Bay of Naples. By the time they'd arrived, Emma had been too jet-lagged and exhausted to do much but look around blearily and collapse into the bed Nico's housekeeper Maria had shown her—a huge, soft kingsized one with views of the sea. His bedroom was adjoining, but the door between the rooms had stayed firmly closed, and after nearly fourteen hours of sleep she'd felt much refreshed and ready to explore.

They'd breakfasted together on yogurt, fresh fruit, and pastries, and then Nico had offered to give her a tour of the island, which Emma had accepted with enthusiasm. After their conversation on the plane the day before, she'd felt reassured they were on the same page when it came to the nature of their relationship. They could be friends, they could even be lovers, but they wouldn't be *in* love. It was an important and necessary distinction, and one Emma was glad she'd made, even as she castigated herself for seeming so arrogant—as arrogant as Nico once had been!—to think he would actually fall in love with her.

Of course he wouldn't, she'd scolded herself when she'd gone to rest in the private jet's sumptuous bedroom during the flight to Rome, and Nico had stayed in the main cabin to work. The reminder had been more for her than for him, not that she'd had any intention of telling him as much. But a man like Nico Santini—rich, powerful, and yes, attractive as all getout, just as she'd told him—wasn't about to fall headlong in love with someone like her, a gutter rat who'd been bounced around so much because no one had ever wanted her enough to keep her. That much was obvious, and it was clear Nico hadn't needed the warning, which was a good thing. Of course it was.

Or so she'd told herself as they'd spent a very pleasant few hours wandering around the island, among the twisted trunks of an ancient olive grove, through the villa's gardens with its climbing bougainvillea and tinkling fountains, down to the sweep of white sand where Nico's private yacht was moored. He'd kept the conversation light and easy, and Emma had relaxed into the chat and banter, grateful that they could enjoy each other's company without having another intense 'getting to know you' talk that she knew she wasn't ready for.

It had been hard, admitting as much as she had, the day before on the plane. She wasn't used to being so vulnerable and tended not to talk about her childhood, the conveyor belt of foster families she'd rotated through, never spending anywhere very long. Except, of course, the last family…she'd spent a whole year with them, in some ways the happiest year of her life… or so she'd thought.

But she definitely hadn't wanted to go into all that with Nico, although perhaps she would one day. In any case, he hadn't asked any invasive questions and she hadn't either, and it had been enough simply to enjoy each other's company, learning little things about him that she hadn't known before—that he liked chess, was scared—or slightly wary, as he'd put it—of spiders, that he'd had a dog growing up and would like one again.

And she'd told him bits and pieces about her own interests that she loved cooking although she'd rarely got the chance to cook much of anything, living in bedsits, that fantasy novels had been her escape of choice as a teen, and she'd never had a pet but thought she might want one one day, although perhaps she'd start small, with a fish or a lizard.

'A lizard!' Nico had exclaimed, laughing. 'They're not very cuddly.'

She'd shrugged, smiling, not wanting to admit that she was a bit nervous to be wholly responsible for a pet. It hardly seemed like a good thing to admit to the father of the baby you were carrying, after all.

'How about a dog and a cat?' Nico had suggested,

his arm around her as they'd strolled back up to the villa for lunch. 'We could teach them to get along.'

'Maybe.' She was still getting used to the whole idea of that *we*; that she and Nico were going to build their lives together. He seemed to have got on board with it remarkably quickly, but Emma knew she needed time to catch up. How could she, who had never known her parents or what it meant to be in a family, build one? *Be* one?

After lunch, Nico excused himself to catch up on work and Emma spent a few hours exploring the villa itself, wandering through its many comfortable rooms, all with views of the sea, and ending up in the cheerful, red-tiled kitchen with the housekeeper, Maria.

'Of course, you must do as you like with the kitchen and food,' Maria assured her while Emma glanced around at the bright copper pans hanging from the ceiling, the bowl of oranges on the table, the ropes of onions and garlic and bunches of herbs hanging from a wooden rafter. 'A woman must always be in charge of her own kitchen.'

'Thank you, that's very kind.' Emma wasn't sure she was confident enough to take charge of a kitchen like this, as much as she liked cooking. Maria seemed more than capable, and she couldn't imagine more or less elbowing her out of the way so she could have a go.

Perhaps she just needed more time, she told herself as she headed upstairs to her bedroom to get ready for dinner. During their walk Nico had encouraged her to think of the villa as her own, and yet she struggled not to feel like a guest, and a temporary one at that.

Nico talked about buying houses and getting pets and she still wondered when he was going to turn around, frown regretfully, and say, *Actually, Emma, this isn't going to work.*

The way everyone else in her life had.

Would she ever get over that deep-seated fear? she wondered as she changed into a pale pink sundress with spaghetti straps. Nico had thoughtfully had an entire wardrobe of clothes shipped to the villa for their arrival, and he'd insisted she keep what she liked and returned what she didn't.

'And I'll need to go to Rome on business soon, so perhaps you can accompany me, and we'll make a shopping trip of it, as well.'

Emma had stammered her thanks, even as the question had hammered through her head: *Why are you being so good to me?* She'd thought it before, and when she'd believed he'd died in that crash, it had almost been as if she'd been expecting it, or something close to it, because when had anything in her life gone right?

And yet now something was. Wonderfully. She really just had to trust it. Lean into it. Let it happen.

It had only been a few days, she reminded herself, and they had weeks, months, maybe even years to get used to each other, to grow. She needed to stop second-guessing herself and enjoy what was right in front of her—Nico included.

Her stomach dipped as she remembered how he'd held her hand as they'd walked through the olive grove, their fingers loosely entwined. How, when he'd helped her over a piece of driftwood on the beach, his hand had spanned her waist and his gaze had briefly, blazingly, met hers. Emma knew Nico meant what he said—he would wait for her to be ready; the ball was firmly in her court when it came to that aspect of their relationship.

And maybe that was the missing piece that would help her feel settled. That would build trust as well as intimacy. That would remind her of how wanted this man made her feel, and how safe.

As long as she kept guarding her heart...

'There you are.' Nico came out onto the terrace, smiling, looking relaxed and rather wonderful in a pale green button-down shirt and dark trousers, his feet bare, his teeth gleaming in his tanned face.

'I was just enjoying the sunset.' She glanced back at the ribbons of lavender and orange that were streaming across the sky as the sun sank towards the placid surface of the sea. 'This feels like paradise.'

'I'm glad.' He brushed her cheek with his fingers. 'You deserve a little paradise.'

Instinctively she tensed at the note in his voice, something she feared might be a bit too close to pity. 'Don't feel sorry for me, Nico,' she warned quietly. 'Because of my childhood or whatever.' She didn't think she could take his pity, not when all she'd ever had was her own strength. She needed to keep it; she couldn't bear for him to feel sorry for her. They wouldn't be equals then; they couldn't be partners.

He raised his eyebrows, his fingers still lingering on her cheek, making it hard to think. To stay strong. 'Do you feel sorry for me?' he asked. 'Because of my childhood...or whatever?'

'Am I supposed to?' she returned tartly, but smiling

too, glad he'd flipped it back on her rather than giving her assurances she wasn't sure she could believe.

'No. Definitely not.' He ran his hand from her cheek to her shoulder and down her arm, twining his fingers with hers. 'If anything, I admire you, Emma, for overcoming so much.' He paused. 'The OB told me some of the things you must have been through.'

She felt a blush heat her cheeks as she imagined what some of those things must have been, the more painful parts of her childhood she'd tried to forget. Why had she agreed, in a moment of defiance, to let her share her medical records with him? 'What kind of things?' she asked, although she wasn't sure she actually wanted him to say it aloud. Still, she wanted to know how much he knew.

'That you'd been malnourished as a child. And that you must have broken your wrist at some point and it didn't heal properly, probably because it hadn't been seen to.' He paused and then added, his voice so achingly gentle, 'And that there were scars on your legs that looked like cigarette burns.'

A lump was forming in her throat, making it hard to speak. Her eyes blurred so the world was just colour—the orange and violet of the sunset, the blue of the sea, the green of Nico's kind, far too kind, gaze. She hadn't expected him to say so much, to know so much. How much had that doctor been able to guess from her determinedly brief answers? 'Well, some of those foster families weren't so great,' she managed in a half-mumble. 'One in particular was pretty bad. But, you know, some were really good…' The ones that hadn't wanted her.

'Oh, Emma.' She couldn't see what he was doing because of her blurred vision, but she felt him. His arms came around her and he drew her softly against him, so her cheek was pressed against his warm, solid chest and she could breathe in the wonderful scent of his aftershave, of *him*. She closed her eyes and a tear slipped down.

'Please don't feel sorry for me, Nico. Really. I don't want you to.'

His hand was warm and steady on her back, moving in slow, comforting circles. 'I told you, I don't. Do you think I should?'

'No, it's just I couldn't stand your pity. I've always tried to be strong—'

'You are strong, Emma. Stronger than you even know.' He eased back, framing her face with his hands, using his thumbs to gently wipe away her tears. 'Stronger than I ever realised.'

'It's hard enough to feel like your equal,' she confessed unsteadily. Maybe that was part of her trust issues—she wondered why he'd want her long-term, when nobody else had. 'I just don't want to feel even more…inferior.'

'Inferior?' His eyebrows rose, his fingers stilling on her face. 'You are far, far from that, in absolutely every way,' he told her, his voice a low, steady thrum, 'I promise you. And I also promise you, as I did before, that I will be there for you in a way those foster families never were. I'll always keep you safe, Emma, I promise.'

His voice throbbed with sincerity as Emma gazed up at him, wondering if she could believe him, longing to yet still struggling—not because of him, she knew, as much as herself. The doubts she still felt. And yet… it was so tempting to believe. She might not want to court the dangers of loving Nico, but living with him as his equal, his friend, and yes, his lover? She realised she wanted that. Desperately.

'Do you believe me?' he asked, and she managed a smile, small and tremulous, but there.

'I'm trying to.'

'How can I convince you?'

As he looked down at her with such tenderness, his hands still framing her face, Emma realised she knew exactly what she wanted—and needed—right now. Not more probing questions or well-intentioned reassurances, which only fed into her doubts and fears, but rather tangible proof—proof that this could work, that *they* could, in the most fundamental and elemental way possible.

'*Well…*' Her smile deepened as she let out an unsteady laugh and let her gaze drop to his mouth before looking up again, a gasp caught in her throat at the gentleness in Nico's eyes darkened with desire. His gaze scanned her face, searching for answers, and she gave them as she lifted her face up for his kiss.

'Are you sure…?' he asked, and she nodded.

'Yes.' Of this, absolutely. There was still so much she was unsure and afraid of—trusting Nico with her heart, whether they could be a family together, whether she could trust herself.

And yet this? Them, together, as one? Yes. She was sure of that. To prove it, she stood on her tiptoes and brushed a kiss across the velvet of his mouth, revelling in the touch and taste of him.

It only lasted a few seconds, but that was all it took. Nico clasped her to him, plundering her mouth with a savage sweetness that thrilled her to her core. Oh, how she'd missed this. She'd let herself forget how good it had been, because it had been easier not to remember, not to miss what she'd had with him, so very briefly.

Although, she acknowledged dazedly, as he blizzarded kisses along her cheek and jaw down to her throat, his mouth moving everywhere with delicious intent, it was even better now, because their relationship was already so much deeper. Built on trust, growing in affection, not some out-of-time fantasy that never would have gone the distance. This, she hoped, would…if she could let herself believe in it.

Somehow they stumbled off the terrace, and into her bedroom. Emma turned to him, her heart hammering with expectation and just a little fear, because her body was different now and, even though everything so far had been absolutely explosive, she still felt unsure. What if he didn't like the changes pregnancy had wrought? She knew she was too thin in some places and she had a very small baby bump, and maybe Nico wouldn't…

That thought was obliterated as he reached for her, pulling the sash of her sundress loose, sliding the skinny straps off her shoulders. Breathlessly, she wriggled free as his own breathing turned ragged.

'You're so beautiful,' he told her softly and Emma let out a nervous little laugh.

'I don't feel beautiful,' she confessed, because she'd

never thought of herself as all that special, and it still amazed her that Nico desired her as much as she knew he did.

'Then let me show you.' He reached out and unclasped her bra, letting the garment fall from her shoulders so she could shrug out of it. Another shrug and the dress, which had caught around her hips, fell to the floor in a puddle of colourful cotton. Nervously, she kicked it away. She was naked save for a pair of bikini briefs, and Nico was still fully dressed. This was feeling a little unequal.

'Feel,' Nico said, and he drew her hand to his chest, so she could feel the thundering beat of his heat under her palm. 'You see what you do to me?' He drew her hand to the buttons of his shirt. 'Will you undress me?'

The question, asked in a rasp of desire, held a vulnerable note that made her ache. It thrilled and amazed her, humbled her too, that he could want her. That he wanted to show her how much. Carefully, her fingers trembling just a little, she unbuttoned his shirt and then spread the fabric apart with her hands, revelling in the feel of his pectoral muscles, perfectly sculpted.

Emma let her hands dance and slide across his chest, exploring every beautiful, burnished inch of him before she dropped her hands to the waistband of his trousers, thrilling even more to the feel of him, yet also suddenly shy.

'You're not going to chicken out, are you?' he teased softly and laughter gurgled in her throat.

'No. Definitely not.' No way was she a chicken, and in truth she was looking forward to this. To all of it. With a flick of her finger she undid the button of his trousers, and then drew down the zip over the impressive, pulsing length of him. A soft groan escaped him as her fingers trailed along his arousal before she pushed his trousers off his hips and he kicked them away, pulling her into his arms to kiss her again, both of them blinded by need.

They half walked, half stumbled, to the bed, limbs entwined, bodies clasped together. Emma didn't think she could ever get enough of him, the feel of him against her, the sense of being both desired and cherished, possessed and protected.

Her head hit the pillow as Nico braced himself on top of her, giving her one blazing look of possession before he bent his head to her breasts. Emma's eyes fluttered closed as he slowly kissed his way down her body, taking his time, enjoying every moment, his hands following the fiery trail of his lips, laughing softly against her skin as a moan escaped her and she arched upwards, silently begging for more, which he gave—and gave.

She didn't think she'd ever get enough, she thought dazedly as she fisted her hands in the dark crispness of his hair and his lips trailed from her navel to even lower as he spread her thighs with his hands and tasted her deeply, making her arch and moan and cry out because it was all so intense, and intimate, and also somehow new. She'd never felt this way before, not even with Nico, and she didn't think anyone else could ever make her feel as much again.

'Nico…' she managed in a half-sob, desperate for release, and he raised his head to brace himself above her as, in one smooth stroke, he entered her at last.

* * *

At last. Nico pressed his forehead to Emma's as he buried himself deep inside her, revelling in the velvety squeeze of her body as she enveloped him, wrapping her legs around his waist to draw him even deeper, so they were completely united, husband and wife—one union, one flesh. He'd never felt this way before—not with any other woman, not even with Emma. This, he realised dazedly, was new.

'Nico...' she said again, a promise, a plea, as she wrapped her arms around him, his whole body pressed to her as if they could fuse their flesh even more together and he began to move, long, assured strokes, each one stoking the flames of his desire higher and brighter, bringing him even closer to her, if such a thing were possible.

Emma met him thrust for thrust, pushing upwards and then drawing him in—higher, faster, hotter, brighter, until, at last, she cried out, convulsing around him as he spent himself, their bodies emptied and yet replete. Nico closed his eyes, overwhelmed not just by the pleasure, intense as it had been, but by the intimacy. What had happened had been profound in a way he could not articulate yet, not even to himself.

He thought—he *hoped*—Emma might feel the same for she didn't speak, no irrepressible laugh or insouciant smile this time. She just put her arms even more tightly around him and pressed her face into his shoulder as the last ripples of their shared climax shuddered through them.

Eventually, Nico didn't know after how long, he

rolled over onto his back and Emma snuggled into him, her breathing slowing so he almost wondered if she was asleep. He slid his hand down her body and she let out a little sigh of contentment. Not asleep, then. Just sated, as he was.

As his palm skimmed her navel, he registered what he hadn't before, in the throes of their lovemaking— the slight swell of her pregnancy. *Their baby.* A thrill ran through him and he kept his hand there, spreading his fingers wide across the bump.

A little bubble of laughter escaped her. 'Is it strange?' she asked, and with his other arm he nestled her more closely against him.

'It's wonderful.'

'Are you…?' She paused, as if choosing her words with care. 'Are you nervous about being a father?'

He considered the question, sensing the hesitation behind it. 'No more than any man, I hope,' he said at last. 'What about you? Are you nervous about being a mother?'

'Yes, kind of.' Her voice sounded small, and he squeezed her shoulders gently in silent reassurance. 'As I told you, I never knew my own mother,' she continued quietly. 'And I didn't really have many examples of good mothers. There was one foster mother…' She stopped, and Nico glanced down at her.

'One?' he prompted gently.

'She was kind,' Emma allowed. 'But…it didn't last.' He sensed there was more to the story, but she clearly didn't want to share it now. 'I just hope I'll know what to do. How to be.'

'We've both had parents who disappointed or failed

us,' Nico told her after a moment, feeling his way through the words. 'But that doesn't have to define us. We can see it as opportunity—opportunity to be the kind of mother or father we never had. A chance to do it better than before, to get it right.'

She was silent for a long moment, weighing his words. 'But what if I can't get it right?' she asked at last, and the fear in her voice made him ache.

'The fact that you're even asking that question tells me you'll try your hardest,' he told her, 'and so will I. And, at the end of the day, that's all either of us can do.'

A little bubble of laughter escaped her. 'You're very wise, you know,' she told him as she tilted her face up to his. 'Don't let that make you any more arrogant than you are, though.'

'I'll try,' Nico promised, and there was laughter in his voice, too. 'Although I am compiling quite a list—rich, powerful, attractive as all get-out, and now wise...'

She punched his shoulder, laughing. 'All right, smarty-pants—'

'Is there anything else you want to add to that list?' Nico asked as he flipped her onto her back and pressed his lips to her throat before moving tantalisingly lower. Emma's eyes fluttered closed as her body became loose-limbed and pliant beneath his touch. He could spend hours exploring every inch of her, he thought as he kissed his way down towards her navel. Days... 'Fantastic lover, perhaps?' he murmured against her skin, and inched lower.

A breathy moan escaped her as her hands raked

through his hair, anchoring him to her. 'I think you know that one already,' she managed unsteadily, and then neither of them spoke for a long time.

CHAPTER TWELVE

EMMA TILTED HER head up to the warm, benevolent sunshine, closing her eyes in pleasure even as her heart fluttered with anticipatory nerves. They'd been cruising up the coast in Nico's private yacht for the last three wonderfully relaxing days, and would be arriving in Civitavecchia that afternoon before heading to his flat in Rome—and real life.

They'd spent the last four weeks on his island, and Emma was reluctant to leave its comfort and safety and face the rest of the world—Nico's family included. No, she acknowledged as she opened her eyes and squinted up at the sun, she wasn't just *reluctant*. She was pretty much terrified. She'd complained that Nico hadn't introduced her to his friends before, but now that he was, she realised she didn't relish the prospect of meeting them, or any of the other guests at the charity gala she and Nico would be attending tomorrow night.

She'd never been to that kind of high-profile event before; in their first month-long relationship, she and Nico had kept to hotels and private restaurants, seeing no one. She'd never had to wear a fancy dress, or mingle with important guests, or act as though she fitted in when she never had before. Why did she think she would be able to now? Why did Nico?

Just thinking about it all made her feel as if an icy pit had opened in her stomach, hollowed her right out. On the island, away from reality, she'd been able—mostly—to keep her old insecurities at bay. Now, as Rome drew ever nearer, they rose in full, clamouring force.

She was a fraud. Nico couldn't possibly want to spend the rest of his life with her. He'd walk away from her, just as everyone else she'd ever cared about had, when he realised what a dud she was.

Not that she wanted to admit any of that to Nico. And not, she knew, that he would give it any credence. But what Nico felt about her away from the rest of the world was surely different from when he had to parade her in public. She'd never been on the kind of display that she would be at this gala, and she was afraid—deeply so—that she wouldn't be up to the challenge. And even more worryingly, that Nico would see that—and agree. Tomorrow night felt like a test, and one she was desperately afraid she would fail.

The last four weeks had been, Emma acknowledged with a pang of nostalgia for what already felt in the past, incredible. It was the same amount of time she'd spent with Nico before the crash, but this time had been, she knew, different in every way. Their previous relationship had been, she realised now, nothing more than a figment, a fantasy, little more than snatched moments in bed in between Nico working, with her always waiting for him to tire of her and the whole thing to end. She'd never shared herself with him, not truly, and he hadn't with her. In comparison, the weeks they'd shared on the island had felt real and total.

They'd spent hours talking, chatting, laughing, sharing, as they'd explored the island, lounged in the garden, or swum in the sea; in the evenings they'd read books, or watched movies, or, more often than not, gone to bed where the pleasures there had continued unabated and deeper and more wonderful still.

Nico had taught her to play chess, and after the first week, Emma had worked up her courage to experiment in the kitchen, whipping up various meals. Nico had delighted in making sure she had whatever ingredients she required for the recipes she wanted to try, whether it was black truffles from France or sundried tomatoes from a farm in Sicily.

It had been fun and even exciting to make the meals they ate together, a form of caring that felt practical, tangible, a way to show him she cared without having to admit it to him—or even herself. And while it was true that not every meal had been a roaring success, Nico hadn't minded, and neither had she, both of them able to laugh at the unmitigated disaster that had been a very crisp sea bass with far too much lemon and garlic. Emma had been glad to return to her love of cooking, yet another avenue of her life that she'd turned away from, all because she'd been afraid to fail.

She'd learned a lot about herself over the last few weeks, and while it had been good, it had also been uncomfortable. Painful, even, to realise her own flaws and failures. In getting to know Nico, and having him get to know her, she'd begun to see the patterns she'd fallen into both as a child and an adult, mainly to guard her own heart. She'd never truly tried at anything, she'd realised, because she'd been so afraid to fail, both with relationships and in life, and she hoped she could be different now. She knew, with Nico, she wanted to be. She just didn't know whether wanting, or even trying, would be enough.

'Enjoying the sun?' Nico asked as he strolled onto the deck from the yacht's main cabin. He was dressed in loose trousers and a white open-neck shirt that made his skin look even more deeply bronzed. The weeks in the sun had only made him more beautiful, his eyes like bits of jade in his tanned face, his white teeth gleaming, and his hair as black as ever.

'I am,' Emma replied, shading her eyes with her hand. She enjoyed seeing him looking so relaxed, so far from the tense, suspicious man who had strode into her wedding. These weeks, she hoped, had been as healing for him as they had been for her. 'How long until we get to Civitavecchia?'

'Another hour, I think.' He smiled wryly as he sat on the deck chair next to her. 'Don't look so thrilled,' he teased.

'I'm nervous,' Emma admitted, although that wasn't even the half of it.

'About seeing my cousin? Trust me, I fully intend to have words with him about how you were treated.'

'I don't want you to fall out with your family,' Emma protested, and Nico shook his head.

'That, I'm afraid, has already happened. Things were tense with Antonio before you even came onto the scene.'

'Well, in any case, it's not that. At least not just that.'

Nico frowned. 'What, then?'

How could she explain it to him? Emma wondered helplessly. How could she make him understand her fear that once they were out in the real world, it would be different? That he would be different, that she would. And the relationship they'd been building would fall apart. Again.

'Whatever it is, Emma,' Nico said, reaching for her hand, 'we'll deal with it... Together.' His smile turned playful as he squeezed her fingers. 'And I hope we'll have fun while we're at it. After a month on a remote island, aren't you looking forward at least a little to getting back to civilisation?'

Emma managed a half-hearted smile back. 'Yes, of course,' she said, although the truth was she'd have been happy to stay tucked away in their own private idyll for ever. But beyond the charity gala, she also had a doctor's appointment and another scan this afternoon, and so the city—and real life—beckoned, whether she was ready for it or not. Whether they were.

An hour later, having changed into a simple tunic-style dress that left room for her ever-expanding bump, Emma disembarked from the yacht with Nico, to the SUV waiting to drive them into Rome for her appointment and scan that afternoon. A week of sun, sleep and good food, as well as plenty of prenatal vitamins and iron had, she hoped, put her back on the road to health both in terms of her weight and her anaemia. She hoped she wouldn't disappoint Nico in that regard, even if tomorrow night's gala turned out to be a disaster.

'I've arranged for you to have some beauty treatments tomorrow,' Nico told her as they drove through the city, a mix of modern buildings, ancient ruins, and pleasant piazzas.

Emma stiffened slightly, although she tried not to show her alarm at such a seemingly innocuous suggestion. 'You have?'

'Yes, I thought you'd enjoy them.' He glanced at her, bemused. Clearly she wasn't doing a good enough job hiding her unease. 'Most women do, don't they? Hair, nails, facials, that sort of thing? I thought it would be a treat for you.'

'Yes, I suppose.' What else could she say? He'd already told her there would be an array of gowns to choose from, brought directly to the hotel, for the gala. She knew she should revel in playing Cinderella for a day, fairy godmother included, but she only felt afraid. Yet another test to try to pass, to fail.

During their whirlwind relationship, she'd always been expecting it to end; even after they married, Emma had wondered how long their relationship could really last. She hadn't let herself get invested, but now, she knew, it was too late.

She might not love Nico—and that was simply because she wouldn't let herself—but she still cared. Too much. She knew she'd be hurt—devastated, frankly— if he changed his mind about her after seeing her fail here in Rome.

And hasn't everyone changed their mind about you?

Why would Nico—rich, powerful, attractive, *amazing* Nico—be any different?

She tried her best to banish that mocking inner

voice and give Nico a smile of gratitude, which he surely deserved. 'Thank you. That's very kind of you.'

His lips twitched. 'Why do I think you had to force yourself to say that?'

He knew her too well, already. 'I'm just not used to any of this,' Emma replied, something of an apology.

He touched her cheek, his smile turning tender, making her eyes sting. No, she really wasn't used to any of this. 'Then this will help you become accustomed,' he told her gently, 'which you'd better—this is the rest of your life, Signora Santini.'

Was that a promise? Emma smiled and tried to believe it, but even as Nico leaned over to kiss her, she knew she couldn't. Not entirely. Life had taught her differently, too many times already.

Nico glanced in the mirror as he twitched the bow tie of his tuxedo, a frown settling between his brows. As much as he'd told Emma he was looking forward to this return to civilisation, the truth was he would have rather stayed on the island, alone with her, lost in a wonderful world of their own making—both in bed and out of it.

As much as he'd enjoyed the earthly delights they'd shared, he'd also found a surprising sweetness in simply spending time with her, whether it was walking, chatting, laughing, or cooking together; he'd jokingly referred to himself as her sous chef, happy to chop or grate while she studied the recipes she was trying with an endearing intensity. He'd loved watching her come alive—the excitement and enthusiasm that brightened her eyes and curved her mouth, the deep laugh that gurgled up when he teased her, far more genuine, he realised, than anything he'd heard from her before. She'd blossomed these last four weeks, he believed, and he was both glad and grateful.

He'd had his own kind of flowering as well, Nico knew, or at least a certain sort of unbending. After being a workaholic for most of his adult life, eschewing serious relationships in order to win his father's approval, he had, for the last four weeks, put his working life more or less on hold in order to spend time with Emma. He'd done the minimum to keep the current business deals with Santini Enterprises going; after his being away for the months after the crash, his father and Antonio had both easily got used to working without him, and Nico found that he actually didn't mind. He had his own private business interests to consider, as well; the investments he'd made with his own money that would, one day he hoped, provide the foundation for an independent business, separate from his family, his past.

After Emma had asked him on the plane what he'd really like to do if he had a choice, he'd realised that of course he *did* have a choice. His father's lack of love and fidelity gave him a freedom he hadn't fully appreciated before, but he realised now that he had no need to stay with Santini Enterprises, that he did not owe his father, or his father's business, any loyalty...

It gave him room to think. To dream, in a way he never had before.

But even with those intriguing possibilities on the horizon, he wanted to focus on Emma, and the life they were building together. The appointment at the OB yesterday afternoon had been as different in every way from the last one as Nico ever could have hoped; he'd sat in on it, for a start, and the doctor had been encouraging about Emma's weight gains and increased iron levels. Best of all, they'd seen the baby kicking and moving on the scan—a truly wondrous sight. He had the printout in his breast pocket; he didn't think he'd ever tire of looking at that blurry form, their baby. Everything had looked healthy and hopeful, and for that Nico was incredibly grateful. No matter what troubles and tragedies surrounded their separate pasts, Emma and his child were the future. Their future.

Smiling at the thought, he went in search of Emma. He found her in the drawing room downstairs, gazing out of the long, sashed window at the view of St Peter's Square. She turned as he approached, and his breath caught in his chest at the sheer loveliness of her. She had, despite her nervousness, enjoyed the beauty treatments—or at least she'd said she had—and the result was that she now looked utterly luminous. Her hair was piled loosely on top of her head, and her skin, dusted with bronzer, glowed with both beauty and health. She lowered her gaze as he walked towards her, a faint blush touching her cheeks.

'I feel like Cinderella,' she told him. 'After the fairy godmother did her "Bibbidi-Bobbidi-Boo" bit.'

'You look like Athena,' Nico replied as he walked across the room and took her hands in his. 'Utterly stunning.' The gown she'd chosen, one of a dozen he'd had ferried over, was an off-the-shoulder piece in bronze satin, its draped folds lovingly nestling her small bump before flaring out around her calves and ankles. 'But there is one thing missing.'

She glanced up at him, amber eyes glowing like embers underneath her dark lashes. 'Missing...?'

'These.' He withdrew a pair of diamond chandelier earrings from his pocket, the stones sparkling in the light; he'd seen them at a jeweller's yesterday and thought they were perfect.

Emma's eyes widened as she took in the magnificent earrings. 'Tell me those are fake.'

'Fake?' Nico raised his eyebrows, smiling. 'You insult me.'

'I can't...'

'You can.' Sometimes he wondered how he could have ever thought she'd only wanted his money. She hardly seemed to use it, always protesting when he lavished her with gifts—clothes, jewellery, anything. Now he helped fasten the earrings, letting his fingers linger on the delicate lobes of her ears.

'You look beautiful.'

'I'm scared I'll do something stupid,' Emma blurted. 'Trip or say something silly... I don't even know.'

'All I want,' Nico assured her, 'is for you to be yourself.'

She shook her head slowly, the earrings nearly brushing her shoulders, her gaze wide and a little panicked. 'This isn't my world, Nico.'

'And I'm glad of it. I like you just as you are, Emma. I don't want you to be some fawning fashionista or boring socialite, whatever it is you have in your head that you think I'm expecting. I want you to be you.' Because, he knew, he was starting to care—very much—

about the *you* she was. If only Emma would let him. Would believe him.

At his words, her lips trembled and her eyes filled. 'I suppose I have trouble believing that,' she told him shakily, 'because no one has ever wanted me to be me before.'

Gently Nico drew her into a hug, resting his chin on top of her head as she pressed her cheek against him. 'We've both had to overcome issues around trust,' he said. Heaven knew he'd had his own. 'But you can believe me, I promise.'

'I know that, really.' With her smile still seeming shaky, she eased out of his embrace. 'I don't want to get make-up on your jacket,' she explained as she turned away. 'And we shouldn't be late.'

'No,' Nico agreed, although he wished he felt more confident that he'd convinced her. He had so much more to say, to proclaim, yet he knew now was not the right time

Twenty minutes later they were stepping into the ballroom of one of Rome's grandest hotels, its floor-to-ceiling windows providing a panoramic view of the city, its elegant confines filled with well-dressed guests. Next to him Emma took a gulping sort of breath and Nico turned to give her a reassuring smile, but she wasn't looking at him.

'It will be fine,' he murmured, and she nodded, tilting her chin and throwing back her shoulders, filling him with pride.

'Right.'

And it was fine, more than fine, Nico realised as

they circulated among the guests. Emma was quiet at first, but then someone asked her something, he didn't even know what, and within minutes she was in an animated conversation with someone about a cooking show, of all things. It made Nico smile.

He looked forward to teasing her about it later. *What did you have to be worried about?* he'd say, and she would give one of her irrepressible laughs and roll her eyes before he took her to bed…

Yes, he was looking forward to that very much. He stood slightly on the sidelines as Emma continued to chat and circulate, enjoying watching her shine. Loving that she was able to be the woman she'd always been meant to be.

Loving her.

The realisation jolted through him. He'd been telling himself all along that what they had worked because they didn't love each other, but now he realised what an absurd fantasy that was. Of *course* he loved her; what was loving, after all, but doing the things he'd done? Feeling the way he felt? Wanting more for her than he wanted for himself? It wasn't some ephemeral will o' the wisp that he could guard against, ward off if he just steeled himself; it was this. Her. Now.

And, he realised as he watched Emma shine, the prospect of loving her, the reality of it, didn't scare him at all. On the contrary, it filled him with hope—and joy. This was what he wanted. And he would tell her, he vowed, at the first opportunity.

CHAPTER THIRTEEN

THIS WASN'T SO BAD, Emma thought as she sipped her drink and smiled and nodded at her new acquaintance—a woman who was as addicted to the Food Network as she was. Her new friend might be worth millions, have a career as a human rights lawyer and a billionaire entrepreneur as a husband, but when it came to rating the best chefs on television, they were equals. A laugh escaped her at the thought, and she clapped her hand over her mouth before she realised she would smudge her lipstick.

As she lowered her hand, her gaze snagged on Nico's—he'd stepped back a bit, content, it seemed, simply to watch, although he was about as far from a wallflower as one could get. Now a faint smile quirked his lips and he raised his champagne glass in a silent, approving toast. To her.

How she loved this man, Emma thought, only to freeze, her mouth dropping open, appalled at the thought. The realisation that was thudding through her, because she'd tried so hard not to love him. Not to love anyone.

The woman she'd been chatting to had moved away,

and Emma took a few steps to the side of the ballroom, her mind spinning with what she'd inadvertently revealed to her own wary heart.

She loved him.

She'd tried to stop it, resist it in every way, stay safe and smart...but he'd breached her defences anyway. With his kindness. And his tenderness. And his willingness to be vulnerable himself. And, she thought as another laugh bubbled up, his being attractive as all get-out—put together, it was an irresistible combination, and her battered heart hadn't been able to stand firm.

Still, she felt incredulous that he'd slipped through her defences without her realising. Torn down her barricades without her realising she was basically handing him the bricks. How had this happened, and how had she let it? And more importantly, far more importantly, what would she do now?

Emma knew her instinct was, as it always had been, to walk away. Run, even.

Don't fail; quit first.

She'd told Nico that had been her unofficial motto, uninspiring as it was, but it was hard not to protect yourself. Not to not want to get hurt. To walk away before someone else did the walking.

And yet...

Did she really want to run away from Nico? Nico, who had shown her so much kindness and passion, tenderness and care? Nico, the father of her child, the guardian of her heart?

No, and that was the scariest thought of all. She *didn't* want to walk away. She wanted—or least was willing—to risk her heart for once, to take this leap into the terrifying unknown. To let herself be as vulnerable as it was possible to be, by telling him she loved him, that she was choosing to believe in the fairy tale they were creating for themselves, moment by precious, tender moment.

But how? When...?

'Didn't you land on your feet?'

The cold, drawling voice had her twanging with tension as Emma slowly turned around. Nico's cousin, Antonio, stood in front of her, looking every bit as derisively mocking as he had the last time she'd laid eyes on him, at Nico's memorial service.

She glanced around the ballroom a bit desperately, hoping for Nico to come to her rescue, but even though she'd only seen him seconds ago he'd somehow disappeared. Where had he gone? Why?

'Hello, Antonio,' she forced out coolly, doing her best not to let her voice tremble. Chin, tilt. Eyes, flash. Face this man down as who he was, cruel and louche. Nothing like Nico.

Are you sure about that?

'So how,' Antonio mused, 'did you manage to snare him a second time? Was it the brat?' He nodded, rather crudely, towards her modest bump. 'Clever, that, especially when he must have been using protection. Nico isn't stupid, after all.'

Emma straightened, stiffening her spine. 'I don't need to talk to you,' she declared in as firm a voice as she could manage, which, she feared, was not firm enough. Not firm at all.

'Do you really think he'll stay with you?' Antonio challenged, his voice turning silky soft. 'For the long term? Oh, I admit he's besotted, it's ridiculous. But do you actually think that will last? Do you think someone like you could actually hold the attention of a man like Nico for all but a nanosecond?' He let out a laugh—high, cruel, utterly derisive. Someone near them glanced over, frowning.

Emma felt a blush scorch her cheeks, but she forced herself to keep Antonio's gaze.

'I feel sorry for you,' she declared. 'You obviously have never been in love.'

'And you think Nico is in love?' Antonio asked incredulously. 'With *you*?'

The question, asked with such blatant, mocking disbelief, caught her on the raw. Opened up all those old, wounded insecurities until she felt as if she were bleeding out. 'Why do you care?' Emma demanded shakily. 'What does it have to do with you?'

He took a step closer to her, looming menacingly close. 'I don't,' he told her bluntly, his scornful gaze raking her from head to toe. 'In fact, I couldn't care less. But I thought you might appreciate some plain speaking. There won't be ten grand for you this time.' He turned away without another word, while Emma was left shaken and reeling.

There wasn't a speck of truth in his statements, she told herself as she tottered on wobbly legs to the ladies' powder room. He was just a callous, cynical, *cruel* man who liked to tear people down for the fun of it. She'd known people like that before, all through her life.

And yet his words *hurt*. They exposed the vulnerability she was still trying so hard to hide, the fear that she wouldn't be good enough, that just as before, *always* before, Nico would change his mind, because everyone changed their mind about her…

'Emma? Absolutely not.'

The memory rushed through, scalding her with its shame. If people she'd let herself love, who had loved her, or seemed to, could be so certain about turning their backs on her, why should Nico be any different?

'It's not true,' Emma said aloud, but her voice sounded feeble to her own ears. It sounded doubtful—because she knew she did doubt. As much as she wanted to believe, to *hope*, she couldn't keep herself from fearing the worst—again. Because in the past the worst had always happened to her.

Taking a shuddering breath, Emma dabbed at her eyes and then repaired her make-up, determined not to let Antonio or anyone else see how he'd affected her. Then, with another breath, she straightened, squaring her shoulders, tilting her chin, and heading back out to the party—and the real world.

She'd barely made it a few steps past the powder room when Nico appeared, smiling easily, although a frown settled between his brows as he took in her undoubtedly still stricken expression.

'There you are.'

'Yes.' Emma did her best to smile, but she felt it wobble and slide off her face.

'Emma?' He touched her arm. 'Are you all right?'

'Yes, just tired.' She gave a slight grimace. 'Being on my feet for so long…all this socialising… I'm used to quieter island life now, I suppose!' She tried for a laugh and felt it ring false.

'Do you want to go home?'

Desperately.

'If…if you don't mind.'

His frown deepened, his gaze scanning her face. 'Of course not. Let me just make my apologies.'

Emma nodded woodenly as Nico turned to head back into the party. The sooner she got out of here, she told herself, the better. And yet she was afraid leaving the party wouldn't change the doubts that now clamoured in her own heart.

Nico weaved his way through the guests, intending only to speak to the host of the gala, to make their apologies. He hoped Emma really only was tired; she'd looked so pale and forlorn, even as she'd tried to smile. Perhaps coming to Rome had been a bad idea. Too much rushing about…

'You haven't said hello, cousin.'

Nico halted mid-stride and turned to see his cousin, Antonio, smiling at him pleasantly, although Nico noted that his eyes looked hard. Besides their brief meeting when he'd returned from Jakarta, before haring off to Los Angeles, he hadn't seen his cousin since the accident. Considering how he'd treated Emma, as well as the latent tension that had been simmering between them since his paternity had become known, he hadn't particularly wanted to.

Now Nico inclined his head. 'Antonio.'

'How's your recovery?' Antonio asked, and Nico thought his tone was rather cool. 'Get your memory back?'

'Of the crash? No.' Antonio had asked him how

much he'd remembered from that day, and Nico had confessed it was all a blank. Now, as he took in his cousin's assessing look, he wondered why he was seeming even more distant and guarded. Was it because of Emma, or something else? Something more?

He wasn't about to broach that whole topic now; he needed to get back to her. 'I'll be back in Rome next week,' he said instead. 'To catch up on all that has happened in my absence.' And to tender his resignation so he could start his own company, but he had no intention of talking about that with his cousin, either.

'Of course.' Antonio's lips twisted. 'I've no doubt you're eager to be back at the helm.'

His cousin's sardonic tone gave him pause, and again, more unrelentingly than ever, he felt that odd, tickling sensation at the back of his head, as if everything would make sense if he could just *remember*...

'Nico?' Antonio frowned, his eyes narrowing. 'Why are you looking at me like that?'

'I...'

A memory was slamming into him as he stared at his cousin.

The pilot of the plane, a panicked look on his face, a parachute on his back. *'I'm sorry, signor.'*

Him, alone in the sabotaged plane, no parachute, no idea what to do. The fuel had been let out of the tank...he was flying low over the ocean...

He blinked Antonio back into focus. 'Sorry,' he said stiffly. 'I just...' He could think of no excuse. 'I'll see you next week.'

Antonio nodded tersely and Nico strode away, his mind reeling. *Antonio*... Could it be possible? Was he remembering things correctly? Antonio, his own cousin, had arranged the accident, hired the pilot to sabotage the plane? Had tried to *kill* him?

'Nico?' Emma's soft voice startled him out of his spinning thoughts. 'Are you okay?'

'Yes.' He bit the word off tersely; he could not tell her his concerns—his fears—now. He would not burden her with them, not until he was sure he could trust his memories, not until he knew what to do—and did it. Of this he would be in control. Completely.

They rode in silence back to his town house, Nico barely aware of Emma sitting so quietly next to him, her face turned to the window. When they arrived back home, Emma murmured something about having a bath, and Nico nodded his approval before closeting himself in his study to make some much-needed calls.

Two hours later, he was staring out at the dark night, his face cast into stark relief by a pale sliver of moonlight as the truth thudded through him. This, he realised, changed everything.

CHAPTER FOURTEEN

IT HAD BEEN two days since they'd returned from Rome via Nico's yacht, and what a miserable two days it had been. The journey had been as swift as possible, and Nico had claimed he had pressing business to attend to, leaving Emma alone. Since their return she had moped around the villa while Nico had made himself scarce in his study, intensely occupied, almost seeming to avoid her. No, she realised, bleakly, not almost. Definitely.

He'd skipped dinner both nights, even though she'd made something specially, and come to bed late, after she'd fallen into a restless, unhappy sleep. When she'd dared to ask him if everything was all right, he'd assured her it was—while not meeting her eye. They'd barely spoken since the gala, and Emma was afraid she knew why.

He'd tired of her, just as she always knew he would. And why wouldn't he, when she obviously hadn't managed the gala very well? She'd seen him talking to Antonio right before they'd left—had his cousin been dripping yet more poison into his ear? Poison that had obviously convinced Nico, since he was determined to keep her at arm's length.

Yet what could she do about any of it? In the past, Emma would have cut and run. She'd long ago learned not to wait around to be given the boot. Leave before someone made you, that had been her *modus operandi*, and it was her instinct to do the same now— an instinct she resisted.

She'd *changed*, hadn't she? She'd learned and grown and fallen in love. It seemed almost absurd that she'd realised she loved Nico just as he was realising the opposite about her, and yet even now, when her heart felt as if it were being rent in two, Emma knew it was true. She loved him. And if she truly loved him, she wouldn't run away as soon as things got a little dicey. A little tough.

No, what she'd do instead was confront him. Tell him how she felt. The prospect, which had already been terrifying, felt even more so in light of Nico's coolness towards her, and yet perhaps that made it all the more necessary. She'd stand her ground this time, Emma told herself even as she quaked at the thought. She'd fight for the hope of their family, of them. For love.

It took another endless, miserable day of Nico avoiding her before she managed to tiptoe up to the door of his study where he'd been closeted since early that morning, hand poised to knock. Her heart was thundering in her chest but before she summoned the courage to tap at the door, she heard Nico's voice. He must be talking on the phone, she realised.

'I want it done immediately,' he said, sounding more tersely clipped than she had ever heard him before.

'Immediately, do you understand? Absolutely no de-lays.'

No delays to *what*? Her hand hovered by the door as she strained to hear.

'Emma?' The surprise in Nico's voice made her tense. 'No, absolutely not. Absolutely *not*.'

Emma stumbled back as his words reverberated through her—the same words she'd heard a lifetime ago, when she'd been only ten years old, listening at the door of the kitchen as her foster mum had spoken on the phone to her care worker. Back then Emma had felt as if her heart had broken, but it was nothing to how she felt now. *Shattered.* Completely and utterly shattered, her heart nothing more than a handful of broken bits.

Blindly, without even knowing where she was going, she whirled around. Headed up to her bedroom and pulled out a duffel bag from the cupboard, started stuffing things into it. None of the clothes Nico had bought her, no, she'd take nothing of his. Just her own things, shabby as they were.

You're back where you started, Emma, are you really surprised?

Yes, she was, and that was the hardest thing. She'd given up on her own principles of staying smart and safe by falling in love—and look where it had landed her.

Dashing the tears from her eyes with an angry hand, she hurried out of the bedroom, and then slipped down the stairs and out of the front door. As she'd packed, she'd considered her plan—how to get off this island without Nico knowing, because she knew she couldn't bear to face him. Whether it was pity or contempt, she didn't want to see it on his face. She just wanted to go.

She'd get the groundskeeper, Maria's husband, Stefano, to take her in Nico's boat—not the yacht they'd taken to Rome, but the little motorboat he used to get supplies from Capri or the mainland. She'd come up with an excuse, or maybe she'd just beg, but somehow she'd get away.

Of course, it wasn't as easy as that. First she had to find Stefano, who was in the gardens, and then stammer out some story about how she wanted to go to Naples for some ingredients for dinner, and would Stefano take her? She knew it was at least an hour's trip, and before she'd finished her plea Stefano was frowning and shaking his head.

'I do not know, *signora*. It is a long way to go, and the waters, they are very choppy.' He smiled kindly. 'What ingredients do you need? I am happy to get them for you.'

'I want to go myself,' Emma insisted as tears started in her eyes, knowing she sounded like a child. 'Please,' she whispered, and Stefano patted her hand.

'If it is so important to you, okay. I will go. Just let me get my things.'

Relief coursed through her. 'I'll meet you down by the boat.'

He nodded, and she hurried down to the dock, her heart still thundering. Just a few more minutes and then she'd be away. Why did that prospect make her feel worse than ever?

For a second Emma hesitated. She could go back to Nico, ask, even demand, what he'd meant. After everything they'd shared, surely she deserved an honest answer? And yet even as she considered such an option, Emma knew she didn't have the strength to go through with it. She couldn't bear to hear from Nico's lips how he didn't love her, didn't want her. It had been bad enough hearing it on the phone. Remembering how discarded she'd felt, how utterly rejected…

Again.

Emma glanced up at the path that wound from the dock to the villa, squinting in the hope of seeing Stefano coming back, ready to go. But as a distant figure came ever closer, she felt as if her once thundering heart was now suspended in her chest. For it wasn't Stefano coming back with the keys, but Nico, walking towards her with long-legged, purposeful strides—and he looked furious.

When Stefano told him that Emma was asking to go to Naples, Nico was both surprised and alarmed. After spending the better part of three days in a state of high tension, with a migraine constantly threatening to swoop down on him, this was the last thing he needed.

He needed Emma to stay on the island, safe and protected, until the matter of Antonio was completely settled. He rose from his desk, trying to moderate his voice as Stefano gazed at him unhappily.

'I thought it was okay, *signor*?' he asked, twisting his hands together. 'The *signora*, she can go where she pleases?'

'Yes, of course she can. But not today. I'll explain it to her, Stefano.'

'She—she had a bag with her,' Stefano ventured nervously, and Nico frowned at him.

'A bag?'

'With…with clothes.' The groundskeeper hung his head, as if he wished he could take back the words.

It took Nico a few stunned seconds to realise what the man meant. Emma had been planning to *leave* him.

The first thing he felt was hurt, a deep, deep abiding pain in his chest, in his heart, but his old instinct rose to the fore and he pushed it away. No, he wasn't hurt. He was angry. Angry that after everything they'd had together, she was going to creep away like a thief in the night? How dared she? Had he been wrong about her after all, all this time?

'I'll take care of it,' he snapped, and Stefano nodded before hurrying away. Nico made his way down to the dock, his anger building with every second. Why would Emma leave him like this? How could she treat him this way, sneaking off without so much as a word?

Why are you surprised? She was willing to marry the next man just months after your supposed death.

No, he told himself, he wasn't going to think like that. Not any more. And yet it was hard not to, when the evidence was there right in front of him, Emma cowering with a duffel bag stuffed with her clothes, before she tilted her chin and glared at him.

'I'm going, and you can't stop me.'

Nico came to a halt on the dock and folded his arms. 'You didn't think you could at least inform me that you were leaving?' he asked in a silky voice that belied his anger, his hurt.

'Why should I?' she threw at him in challenge, with

all of her old spirit and courage. 'I'm just saving you the time, Nico.'

Nico stared at her—noticing how tightly she clutched her bag, her wide, frightened eyes, the way she bit her lips. No, she hadn't said that with her old, feisty spirit, only the fading façade of it. He took a step towards her and then stopped, because she seemed so wild, so desperate. Why?

'Saving me time?' he enquired. 'How so?'

'You...you know how.'

He shook his head. 'I really don't.'

'Why are you making me say it?' she cried. 'It was bad enough to hear it on the phone—'

'On the phone?' He frowned as he realised she must have heard him talking—did she realise what Antonio had done? Was she blaming him somehow? 'Emma, whatever you heard—'

'What I heard is you wanting to divorce me as soon as possible. With no *delays*.'

'What?' Nico couldn't keep from goggling at her. 'Emma—'

'Look, I've been left a lot in my life, okay? I know when things are starting to go south, and I try not to stick around. So spare me the post-mortem and I'll be on my way—'

'No, absolutely not.'

'That's what you said!' she exclaimed, her tone turning shrill, desperate. '"Emma? Absolutely not." I *heard* you, Nico.' Her voice broke on his name and everything in him ached with remorse.

'You might have heard those words, Emma,' Nico said as gently as he could, 'but you came to conclusions that were, I promise you, entirely wrong.' He glanced at the boat, the wind picking up that was ruffling the water, and then reached for her arm.

She jerked away. 'Don't—'

'Please, let's talk about this rationally, back in the house.' He longed to take her in his arms, but he kept himself from it, at least for now, when she would only resist. 'I can explain everything, Emma, I promise.'

She stared at him, tears filling her eyes, one slipping down her cheek and making his heart break. He'd caused this. He'd fed into her insecurities because he'd been too proud to explain everything properly, to admit how he'd failed, by not remembering. By not keeping her safe, as he'd vowed. By not wanting to admit that his family had turned on him utterly, rejected him more than he'd ever imagined. He'd been arrogant and autocratic, he realised, just as she'd teasingly accused all those weeks ago, and all to hide his own pain—a pain he should have shared with her, instead of trying to handle it on his own.

'Emma,' he said softly. 'Please.'

'I trusted you, Nico.' Her voice was soft and sad. 'I—'

She stopped abruptly, and, with a thrill of hope, he wondered if she'd been going to say she loved him— as he loved her. How he'd wanted to tell her, and yet this business with Antonio had completely taken him over, body and soul. He hadn't wanted to say the words to her until he could be sure he could keep her safe. Until their futures were secure.

Until he had no weakness to admit.

He'd told himself it made sense, but he knew now

it had been nothing more than pride. Pride—just as his father had clung to his pride. Not wanting to be humiliated, to be seen as weak, the object of pity, because his own cousin had tried to kill him and was still walking free.

Gently he reached for her arm again. 'Please, can we talk?'

After what felt like an age but was only a few seconds, Emma bit her lip and nodded. 'All right,' she whispered. 'We can talk.'

He clasped her hand in his as they walked back to the villa in a silence that felt more resigned, at least on Emma's part, than tense or angry. He wondered if he could convince her. He knew he needed to.

'So what is there really to say?' she asked without preamble when they were both in the villa's drawing room, its French windows open to the terrace that looked out to the sea.

'There is a lot to say, as it happens.' He took a steadying breath, determined to stay reasonable. Understanding. 'But it would help first if you'd tell me what you thought I said, on the phone. What you thought I meant.'

Her eyes filled with tears again and she blinked them back angrily. 'Wasn't it obvious?'

'Not to me.'

'You were going to divorce me. Or send me away. Or—something.' She hunched her shoulders, folding her arms, as if she could keep out the whole world.

Nico's heart ached for the woman before him, who had been rejected so many times she didn't trust love when it was staring her in the face. And why should

she, when he hadn't been humble and brave enough
to tell her?

'I wasn't, Emma,' he said gently. 'I had no intention
of doing any of those things, because I—I love you.'

Her eyes widened and her lips parted but she said
nothing, just stared at him, and so he continued, 'I
should have told you before. I wanted to, but—events
overwhelmed me. Events I'll explain in a minute. But
the important thing is, the only thing really is, I love
you. I realised it at the gala, watching you shine. Seeing you be the woman I've known you could be, the
woman at my side whom I love, the woman who makes
me the man I want to be. Or at least, to try. I realised it
then, at the gala,' he amended, 'but I fell in love with
you before. Not in a single moment, but over time—
time that I spent with you. And I know we agreed that
love was off the table, but what is love, if not this?' His
voice rose in challenge. 'You and me together, enjoying
each other's company, caring about the other person,
wanting the best for them, no matter what it is? Isn't
that love? Not some ephemeral fairy-tale feeling, but
reality. Action. Fact.'

A tiny, incredulous smile quirked her mouth. 'That
was quite a speech.'

He let out a shaky laugh, because the truth was he
felt incredibly vulnerable for admitting for so much,
when she hadn't said she loved him yet. Considering
her actions today, maybe she wouldn't. 'Thank you,'
he managed. 'I meant every word.'

Emma stared at him, unfortunately looking far from
convinced. 'Why have you ignored me for the last
few days?' she asked. 'Shut me out, ever since the

gala? And what were you talking about on the phone, if not that?'

'I didn't mean to ignore you,' Nico told her. 'Although I accept that is how it looked and felt. I was very much consumed with—a business matter.' Some business matter, he thought, and yet even now he was reluctant to admit to her what had happened. How he had been betrayed.

Her eyebrows rose. 'A *business* matter?'

'At the gala,' Nico confessed slowly, 'my memory came back. From the crash.' Emma's eyes widened once more and he continued more resolutely, knowing he needed to be honest, 'I remembered being on the plane. It had been deliberately sabotaged. The pilot emptied the fuel tank and then parachuted out. I confronted him before he jumped he told me he was sorry, and that...that Antonio, my cousin, had arranged it all.'

'What...?' The word came out in an incredulous breath. 'Nico, is that true? I'm so sorry.'

'I shouldn't have been as surprised as I was, perhaps. I always knew Antonio was rather ruthless, just as he was with you. And knowing he was truly a Santini and I wasn't, yet my father was still keeping me on as CEO... I knew it had hit him hard. Very hard, to plot my murder.' He tried to smile wryly but didn't manage it. Even though there had quite clearly been no love lost between him and his cousin, yet another betrayal had been hard to bear. Still was.

And isn't that at least part of the reason you didn't tell Emma?

Because he'd been ashamed, how comprehensively

his family had rejected him. Because it had made him feel unlovable…just as she had felt for so long.

'That phone call was me talking to the private investigator, telling him I didn't want you to have to be involved or called as a witness in any way. I wanted to keep you out of it for your own sake, but… I shouldn't have made that decision unilaterally, and I certainly shouldn't have shut you out the way I did. I'm sorry, Emma,' Nico told her, meaning it utterly. 'I should have told you about it all. I shouldn't have kept so much from you for so long. I just…' He spread his hands helplessly. 'I wanted to handle it by myself. And I didn't want to admit I hadn't been able to. Or that my family had turned on me so thoroughly.'

'Oh, Nico.' She took a step towards him, her face softened with compassion. 'I, of all people, can understand that. The reason your phone call hit me so hard was because you used the exact words my foster mother did, when I was ten years old.' She took a careful breath. 'I told you there was one family above all the others that I cared about but I didn't tell you exactly what happened. I'd been there for a year… what felt like the happiest year of my life. They were so kind, and they really treated me as one of the family. Proper, you know? Real.' She bit her lip and then continued quietly, 'My case worker hinted that they might adopt me. In retrospect she shouldn't have said as much, but I think she wanted to give me some hope, and maybe she thought it was a sure thing. But I overheard my foster mum on the phone with her, and when she suggested adoption my foster mum said, "Emma? Absolutely not."'

She gulped a little, and Nico knew how much this still had to hurt.

'She was so certain, you know? And so...so scandalised. Like she never would have entertained the prospect for so much as a second. Well, I started acting out after that, I know I did, and I was gone within a couple of weeks. I never told her I'd overheard. I never asked why.'

'Oh, Emma.' He reached for her then, and she came into his arms with a small, unhappy sigh.

'When I heard you saying the same thing, it was like I'd gone back in time. I guess I went a little crazy,' she admitted unsteadily. 'All I could think about was how it had been before, and not having that happen again. Funnily enough...' She eased back, tilting up her face to look at him. 'I was coming to the study to confront you. To ask you why you were keeping your distance, and to tell you I loved you.'

Nico's grip tightened on her as his heart leapt. 'You were?'

'Yes. I realised it the night of the gala, as well. Maybe it was seeing you with so many other people... I realised how much.' She smiled shyly. 'I felt we belonged together.'

'We do.' His voice was fervent, and her smile turned playful.

'You're sure?'

'More sure of that than anything else in my life.'

Her expression turned serious as her arms tightened around his waist. 'And Antonio? What...what will happen with him?'

'It's being dealt with,' Nico told her soberly. 'It's

what I've been dealing with for the last few days—hiring an investigator, getting evidence. He's being taken in for questioning today.'

'Oh, Nico. Your own cousin…'

'I know.' He swallowed, still finding it hard to bear, to believe, even after several days of thinking of little else. 'I knew he was ruthless, but I never thought him capable of such a thing. I… I loved him.' He bowed his head. 'And I suppose that was part of why I didn't tell you. I felt…ashamed, somehow, I suppose…that someone I loved would do that to me.'

'I know how that feels,' she whispered, and then gave him an impish smile. 'Although not the killing part.' Her expression grew serious again. 'But feeling rejected by the people you care about, who you thought cared about you?' she asked quietly. 'Yes.'

He knew she did, and he was grateful for her understanding and compassion. Nico pressed his lips to her forehead, closing his eyes as he silently thanked providence for bringing her into his life. 'We have more in common than we could have ever known,' he murmured.

'Definitely more in common,' she teased, placing his hand over her bump. 'Feel.'

To his amazement and joy, he felt a flutter against his palm—a tiny foot or hand kicking against him. He laughed aloud, and then so did Emma.

Nico gathered her into his arms, kissing her thoroughly. 'We have the future ahead of us,' he told her. 'All of it to look forward to, together.' He paused to kiss her again, smiling down at her, full of gratitude and joy. 'The three of us.'

EPILOGUE

One year later

'YOUR DAUGHTER HAS a strong pair of lungs.'

Nico came into the kitchen with a six-month-old baby on his hip, with a head of black curls and golden, long-lashed eyes. And she was screaming at the top of her lungs.

'Our daughter, you mean?' Emma teased as she took the baby from him and gave her a smacking kiss on the cheek. 'Thea just knows what she wants.'

'And right now she wants her mama,' Nico replied ruefully as Thea settled right down.

Emma laughed and leaned over to kiss him on the cheek, as well. 'She just wants her nap. I'll put her down now before I finish this.'

'You look like you're in the middle of something,' he remarked, glancing around at the pots and pans bubbling away on the stovetop.

'Nothing that can't wait.' Three months ago Emma had, with capital from Nico's new business, started her own private catering company. Based in the country house they'd bought in Tuscany, she provided meals for dinner parties and private occasions. She'd only had a few bookings so far, which was fine, since Thea was so young, but the business looked set to grow, just as Nico's did.

The last year had been one of beginnings— learning to be husband and wife, and then to be parents. Learning to let go of the family they'd lost— Antonio was in prison, and Nico was no longer in contact with his father—and finding their new support system. Maria and Stefano had moved from the island to Tuscany with them, and served as honorary grandparents, emergency babysitters, and much-valued friends.

All in all, it was a life Emma never would have dared dream for herself—a life of love, of happiness, of warmth and sharing and joy. Not that it had all been easy; the old insecurities sometimes rose to the fore for both of them, and it took patience and honesty and that difficult willingness to be vulnerable to work through it. But they had and they continued to do so, and for that Emma was very grateful.

'After you put Thea down...' Nico suggested hopefully, wiggling his eyebrows with playful suggestiveness '...maybe you want to have a nap yourself...?'

Emma glanced around at the pots and pans, pursing her lips. Yes, in this instance, it certainly could all wait.

'I might,' she agreed thoughtfully. 'I *am* rather tired...'

Nico's face fell just a little and she laughed, a

sound of complete joy, before she ran up the stairs with her daughter giggling all the way, Nico fast behind her.

* * * * *

Couldn't get enough of
Back to Claim His Italian Heir?
Then you'll love these other Kate Hewitt stories!

Claiming My Bride of Convenience
The Italian's Unexpected Baby
Vows to Save His Crown
Pride & the Italian's Proposal
A Scandal Made at Midnight

Available now!

#4121 THE MAID MARRIED TO THE BILLIONAIRE
Cinderella Sisters for Billionaires
by Lynne Graham
Enigmatic billionaire Enzo discovers Skye frightened and on the run with her tiny siblings. Honorably, Enzo offers them sanctuary and Skye a job. But could their simmering attraction solve another problem—his need for a bride?

#4122 HIS HOUSEKEEPER'S TWIN BABY CONFESSION
by Abby Green
Housekeeper Carrie wasn't looking for love. Especially with her emotionally guarded boss, Massimo. But when their chemistry ignites on a trip to Buenos Aires, Carrie is left with some shocking news. She's expecting Massimo's twins!

#4123 IMPOSSIBLE HEIR FOR THE KING
Innocent Royal Runaways
by Natalie Anderson
Unwilling to inflict the crown on anyone else, King Niko didn't want a wife. But then he learns of a medical mix-up. Maia, a woman he's never met, is carrying his child! And there's only one way to legitimize his heir...

#4124 A RING TO CLAIM HER CROWN
by Amanda Cinelli
To become queen, Princess Minerva must marry. So when she sees her ex-fiancé, Liro, among her suitors, she's shocked! The past is raw between them, but the more time she spends in Liro's alluring presence, the more wearing anyone else's ring feels unthinkable...

HPCNMRA0623

#4125 THE BILLIONAIRE'S ACCIDENTAL LEGACY
From Destitute to Diamonds
by Millie Adams

When playboy billionaire Ewan "loses" his Scottish estate to poker pro Jessie, he doesn't expect the sizzling night they end up sharing... So months later when he sees a photo of a very beautiful, very *pregnant* Jessie, a new endgame is required. He's playing for keeps!

#4126 AWAKENED ON HER ROYAL WEDDING NIGHT
by Dani Collins

Prince Felipe must wed promptly or lose his crown. And though model Claudine is surprised by his proposal, she agrees. She's never felt the kind of searing heat that flashes between them before. But can she enjoy the benefits of their marital bed without catching feelings for her new husband?

#4127 UNVEILED AS THE ITALIAN'S BRIDE
by Cathy Williams

Dante needs a wife—urgently! And the business magnate looks to the one woman he trusts...his daughter's nanny! It's just a mutually beneficial business arrangement. Until their first kiss after "I do" lifts the veil on an inconvenient, inescapable attraction!

#4128 THE BOSS'S FORBIDDEN ASSISTANT
by Clare Connelly

Brazilian billionaire Salvador retreated to his private island after experiencing a tragic loss, vowing not to love again. When he's forced to hire a temporary assistant, he's convinced Harper Lawson won't meet his scrupulous standards... Instead, she exceeds them. If only he wasn't drawn to their untamable forbidden chemistry...

YOU CAN FIND MORE INFORMATION ON UPCOMING HARLEQUIN TITLES, FREE EXCERPTS AND MORE AT HARLEQUIN.COM.

HPCNMRB0623

HARLEQUIN
PLUS

Try the best multimedia subscription service for romance readers like you!

Read, Watch and Play.

Experience the easiest way to get the romance content you crave.

Start your **FREE TRIAL** at
www.harlequinplus.com/freetrial.